olivia

ROSIE RUSHTON

hyperion
new york

First American Edition 2000
    3 5 7 9 10 8 6 4
ISBN: 0-7868-1392-X
LIBRARY OF CONGRESS CATALOG CARD NUMBER: 99-6819

Visit www.hyperionteens.com

contents

olivia
reflects

livia Hunter was of the firm opinion that her face was too round, her hair too frizzy and her nose too freckled. Staring at her reflection in the Year Nine locker room mirror, it occurred to her that it was extraordinarily unfair that these physical attributes, all of which she had inherited from her father, should give him a look of boyish charm and her the appearance of a small rice pudding. Despite reassurances from her friends that she was very pretty, had wonderful cheekbones and exquisitely tapering fingers, Livi, as everyone called her, saw only that her two front teeth were slightly askew and that her boobs were disappointing by their absence.

The fact that her hair was the sort of honey blond that most people spend hours bent over the bath with two bottles of dye and a pair of rubber gloves in the hopes of achieving, and that no one noticed her few freckles because they were too busy being mesmerised by her huge pale violet eyes, she chose to ignore. Her skin was so transparently fair that it gave a whole new meaning to being pale and interesting, and when she smiled, her chin dimpled endearingly, a characteristic that throughout junior school had been her saving grace with a number of teachers who felt they couldn't really reprimand someone so cute. But Livi wasn't interested in cute. She wanted to be alluring.

It was a source of enormous worry to her that in all her fourteen years, she had not managed to keep a boyfriend for more than five weeks and three days, which she saw as evidence that she was totally without appeal and would probably end up a shrivelled old spinster with only cats and rubber plants for company.

She turned her profile to the mirror and sighed deeply. The streaks that she had applied with such care from a box of Streak Me Softly Highlights-To-Go were too thin and looked, she thought, like faded shoelaces at the side of her head. The funky sunflower barrette that had looked so cool on the model in last month's *Yell!* magazine had not gone down at all well with Miss Plover, who had requested its immediate removal, with the result that Livi's hair was now held in place with a metal hairgrip, which was about as naff as you could get. Never mind a bad hair day; Livi Hunter was having a bad everything day.

"Hey, Livi, hurry up—it's ten to two!" Hayley Spicer flicked some lip gloss across her mouth and grabbed her bag. "You know what a state old Jollity gets into if anyone's late for her lessons."

"I know, I'm coming," sighed Livi, yanking her hair behind her ears and then thinking better of it. She peered angrily at a minute blackhead in the middle of her chin and snarled.

"You're not getting ready for a date, you know; it's only PSE!" sneered Abigail Lane, slamming her locker door and following Hayley into the corridor.

This was easy for Abigail to say, since she had shoulder-length chestnut hair that bounced like a shampoo advert, the longest eyelashes in the school, and was going out with Adam Reilly, after whom Livi had been lusting since he and his twin sister, Tasha, had started at Bellborough Court the term before. Adam was utterly divine; he had indigo-coloured eyes and skin the colour of very milky coffee, and every girl in Year Nine had fancied him. So Livi had been totally over the moon when at Melissa Field's eighteenth birthday party, he had told her that violet eyes were ultra sexy, and proved it by giving her a long, lingering kiss behind Mrs. Field's prize fuchsias. Sadly, in the weeks that followed he appeared to have been charmed by the variously coloured eyes of a whole clutch of Year Nine girls, and was now firmly under the spell of Abigail's green-eyed gaze. Livi had asked him what she had done wrong—even though all her friends had told her quite firmly not to show any signs of distress at being dumped—and he had given her the old spiel about really liking her, but not thinking they were quite right for one another. Nobody, she thought miserably, considered her right for them.

It wasn't as if she didn't try. She followed all

the Get a Guy tips in *Yell!* magazine even when it meant pretending to be interested in football and stock car racing. Poppy, who was Melissa's sister and had been Livi's best friend since playgroup, said that her lack of success was down to her not being aloof and mysterious enough, but Livi thought it was because of the freckles and having fat thighs and a mother who was too mean to buy her cool gear. And now Adam had gone off with Abigail, who was useless at schoolwork but brilliant at pouting and posing. Livi had practised pouting; it simply made her look sulky and when she tried smouldering glances, people asked if she had something in her eye.

School, thought Livi, scrabbling in her locker for her PSE folder, was just not the same without Poppy. She had left Bellborough Court at the end of last term because her dad's business had collapsed and he could no longer afford the fees. The only reason Livi was there was because she had won a music scholarship and everything was free and sometimes she wished she hadn't because then she would be at Lee Hill comprehensive with Poppy. When the Fields had sold their big house and moved into a pair of old cottages at Canal End, Livi was the first to offer Poppy comfort and consolation. Livi knew all about downshifting. The Hunters had been forced to sell their old Victorian rectory two years before when her dad lost three jobs in a row, and had moved into a red brick Edwardian terrace which the estate agent called "full of character" and Livi called poky. Not that Poppy had needed much support; she had seemed hardly fazed at all by the upheaval of moving house and switching schools—but then, very little fazed Poppy. Which was why Livi had leaned on her and why she missed her so much. It was as if a part of her were missing.

"You've got other friends," her mother had said in that dismissive way in which parents respond when they can't think of a way to make things better. "There's Hayley and Tamsin . . ."

"But they're not Poppy!" Livi had protested. "Poppy was comfortable!" And after she had said it, she had realised that that was exactly it. She really liked Hayley, and spent a lot of time with her. But being friends with Hayley meant hanging out with Tamsin and the oh-so-cool Abigail as well, and somehow Livi always felt she had to work hard to keep up with the leading lights of the "in" crowd. They never seemed to get uptight over anything and tended to look down on anyone who wasn't mega hip and totally committed to having a good time at all costs. But with Poppy, Livi never had to pretend. When Livi's dad had upped and left to live in Runcorn with the Wretched Rosalie, and her mum had made mood swings into an art form and taken to sitting cross-legged on the floor listening to pan pipes and burning incense cones, Livi had poured out her troubles to Poppy who, appropriately for one who intended becoming the country's youngest agony aunt, had told her exactly what to do and how to handle it. Her schemes hadn't always worked, but having her to talk to made the problems her parents kept hurtling at her that much easier to bear.

And with parents like hers she needed all the help she could get, she thought, stuffing her folder into her bag and heading off across the courtyard. When her dad had first left home,

Livi, encouraged by Poppy's unfailingly optimistic outlook on life, had let herself believe that it was just a phase. She had read up on mid-life crisis and comforted herself with the thought that her father was bound to come to his senses and get bored of living with a woman with a big nose and absolutely no dress sense, and come home to Mum, who might be a bit scatty and temperamental, but who wouldn't be seen dead in leopardskin leggings and sweaters with sequins on the front. Then Mum would stop being maniacally happy one moment and morbidly miserable the next, and everything could go back to being as it was.

But as time went on, Livi began to wonder whether her dad really cared about either of them at all. It seemed as if now the only person who mattered to him was Rosalie. It was that wretched woman's fault that Livi hadn't seen her dad in ages. He had promised to come two weeks before, but Rosalie's car had broken down and he had to take her to her aquarobics class.

"I hope she drowns," Livi had muttered.

And then last weekend, on the evening

before he was due to take her to Sunday lunch at The Snooty Fox, he had telephoned to say that Rosalie had a migraine and he couldn't possibly leave her.

"Why not?" Livi had asked curtly. "All she has to do is lie flat in a darkened room; she doesn't need you there to do that."

"Well, she needs me around to help," her father had replied nervously.

"How totally wet!" retorted Livi. "Anyway, the migraine will be gone by the morning."

"Oh, I doubt it very much," said her father hastily. "She suffers dreadfully with her head."

"Probably because there's nothing inside it!" Disappointment always made Livi acerbic.

"Olivia! Don't be so childish—you hardly know Rosalie. You are simply not being fair!"

"Fair? Fair?" Livi had struggled against a sudden impulse to burst into tears. "Oh, and I suppose it's fair that you left us to go and live miles away with her? I suppose it's fair that you keep breaking your promises to me because she matters more than I ever could? Well, don't come; I don't care whether I see you or not."

And she had slammed down the phone before he could say another word.

But she did care. She cared a lot. Not just about the missed lunch, but about the fact that he would rather be with Rosalie, who was quite obviously a blatant seductress and up to no good at all, than with his own daughter who loved him to bits.

She cared that her mum, who hadn't done anything wrong, was having to work flat out and always looked tired, while Rosalie probably spent all her time going swimming and having coffee mornings.

"I bet she didn't even have a miserable migraine," Livi had moaned to Hayley while they were eating their sandwiches in the school cafeteria that lunchtime. "It's probably just a ruse so that she gets to keep Dad all to herself."

"She won't last," Hayley had reassured her, rapidly demolishing a cheese and tomato roll and wiping mayonnaise off her chin. "Your dad hasn't asked for a divorce, which means that subconsciously he knows that he is better off with your mum. He's just having a fling—it'll pass.

Male menopause," she added knowledgeably.

Hayley's parents had divorced and both had married again, with the result that Hayley's extended family read like the family tree of the crowned heads of Europe. She had so many half-brothers and stepsisters that Livi got totally confused as to who was who.

But Hayley was right, thought Livi as she ran up the corridor to Room 18. Maybe Dad would soon get fed up with a woman who couldn't even handle a headache on her own, and the next time he came, he would look at Mum with new eyes and fall madly in love with her all over again. Not that her mother was, in Livi's opinion, making enough of an effort to woo her father back. Whenever he phoned, all Judy Hunter talked about was bills that needed paying or the fact that there was a damp patch on the bathroom ceiling. The last time Dad had come down, Judy had greeted him at the front door dressed in clay-splattered dungarees and rubber gloves, which was hardly likely to arouse erotic thoughts in her father's mind. Livi had tried explaining to her in some considerable detail that Clarissa Carradine in *Lovelines* magazine said that the secret to getting your man back was to offer him constant reminders of what he was missing. You had to use the full force of your feminine allure, which Clarissa said was a woman's most powerful tool. Livi's mum had responded by saying she would like to see Ms. Carradine being alluring after a run-in with the bank manager and six hours moulding cauldrons for a set of ceramic witches.

Judy Hunter was very artistic and somewhat temperamental and made pottery pixies and terracotta gnomes and sold them at craft fairs. Only, since Dad had left, she had made a lot of weird witches and angry hobgoblins instead, and had discovered a new best-selling line in cross little trolls with their tongues hanging out. She had had a whole new set of business cards printed, referring to her as "Judy Joplin, creator of magic in ceramic and clay," because Judy was experiencing what she called a rebirth, and Livi called incipient insanity. Judy said her maiden name rolled off the tongue more alliteratively than Hunter, but Livi reckoned it was just another sign that she was forgetting Dad far too quickly.

"Olivia Hunter!" Mrs. Joll was standing by the window in Room 18 tapping her burnt umber fingernails on the radiator when Livi burst into the room.

"How good of you to deign to join us! I do hope my intention to hold a class hasn't interrupted some other important consideration in your life?"

The rest of the class tittered. Jollity was known for her sarcasm and it was always amusing as long as it wasn't directed at you.

"Sorry, Mrs. Joll," said Livi meekly. "I was thinking about something and forgot the time."

"Oh, thinking, was it?" mocked Mrs. Joll. "How novel. Well, since the subject of our discussion today is Family Relationships, perhaps you might like to think about that?"

Actually, thought Livi, I'd rather not.

hayley
masterminds
a strategy

"She makes it sound so easy, doesn't she?" mused Livi to Hayley on the school bus that afternoon. "I mean, old Jollity goes on about 'calm discussions' and 'listening to the alternative point of view'—but then she doesn't live in my house."

"Nor mine," agreed Hayley, yanking open a packet of cheese and onion crisps with her teeth. Hayley was plump and pretty and rarely went for more than an hour without a deep desire for food, which she enjoyed with the same verve and enthusiasm that she applied to everything else in life. When Livi had announced that she was going on a cottage cheese and fruit diet in an attempt to slim down her thighs, it had been Hayley who had declared that she was quite insane and that life was too short to count calories and besides, who wanted to look like a stick insect?

She offered Livi a crisp and appeared quite relieved when she refused.

"Clive—he's my stepdad—is totally unreal," Hayley commented cheerfully between munches. "One minute he's playing the all-caring stepfather, the next he's down on me like a ton of bricks. Like yesterday—I called my mum a dork, just in fun, and he went ballistic and told me to go to my room! And my mum hadn't even heard what I called her until he got all aerated over it. Moody or what?"

Livi nodded.

"Tell me about it," she agreed. Her own mother's moods swung from All-Embracing Earth Mother to the Harridan from Hell.

"Well, at least you don't have a stepfamily to cope with," observed Hayley, demolishing the last of the crisps and licking salt off her chubby fingers. "And your mum seems really funky—hardly the type to throw wobblies."

"You have to be joking," protested Livi raising

her eyebrows heavenwards. "You weren't there on Sunday."

It had been bad enough being stood up by her dad, without having a blazing row with her mother. They had been sitting in their bathrobes, peaceably eating croissants and flipping through the Sunday papers, when Judy had suddenly slammed her knife onto the table, pushed back her chair and started pacing up and down the kitchen.

"I could murder that man for dumping on you like that!" she had exclaimed, grabbing her mug and slopping coffee all over the breakfast bar. "But then, why should I be surprised—he's never had any sense of responsibility!"

Whenever her mum starting slagging off her dad, Livi felt her heart beat faster and her stomach lurch wildly as if she were on a rollercoaster. She wanted her mum to remember all Dad's good points, not keep focusing on the odd bad one.

"You know how soft-hearted and caring he is," said Livi hurriedly. "You always used to say that if Dad found a wounded sparrow and a ten pound note on the pavement, he'd use the money to wrap the sparrow in!" She waited for her mum to laugh at this long-standing family joke, but all that was forthcoming was a muttered grunt.

Livi tried again.

"Anyway, I don't suppose he had much choice. I reckon Wretched Rosalie fed him a sob story and he was just doing what he thought was right."

"Oh, undoubtedly," said her mother sarcastically, yanking a diamante barrette out of her freshly dyed amber hair and hurling it onto the table. "It's just a pity that he never seemed to consider it 'right' to pay the bills or remain faithful or actually do any of the things he said he was going to do! But then, that's Mike Hunter for you, all words and no action!"

Livi had known that once her mum got into her stride, this could go on for ever. She hated having to listen to her going on and on about Dad's shortcomings. OK, so he wasn't great with money; when they had to sell their house, he had told Livi that sensitive people are rarely financial wizards and anyway, what did money really matter in the great scheme of things? To which her mother had replied that funnily enough most of the world used it for paying their debts and clothing their kids and certainly not on having office flirtations and sending flowers to juvenile accounts clerks. These exchanges always led to one of those awful shouting matches that ended in Livi's dad storming out of the front door, into his car and straight up the M6 to Runcorn. The rows had got more and more frequent, until one day Dad went to Runcorn and didn't come back.

"And another thing, your irresponsible father . . ." Judy began, slamming her fist on the table.

"Oh, Mum," begged Livi, "don't start!"

"Don't start?" Judy's cheeks flushed pink and her eyes looked suspiciously bright. "Don't start, you say? I never stop! I've got another half dozen witches to make for the Kettleborough Craft Fair next week, and Mrs. Liddington keeps nagging me to finish her Norwegian Troll umbrella stand. I had thought that with you out of the way with your father, I could get a clear run at it all, but now I suppose . . ."

"Oh, terrific!" Livi had yelled, flinging the Sunday supplement on the floor. "So sorry I exist! Don't mind me; I'll just evaporate, shall I?"

And she had stormed out of the kitchen, rushed upstairs, and slammed her bedroom door as violently as she could. She had assumed that her mother would follow, full of apologies for being so unfeeling. She hadn't. Within a few minutes, the sound of pan pipes on her mother's Relax and Revitalise CD wafted up the stairs.

"They don't like apologising," commented Hayley, when Livi relayed the story to her. "It offends their sense of superiority."

"Oh, she came round in the end," said Livi hastily. She didn't mind criticising her parents but she wasn't about to have anyone else do it.

Livi had been on the point of telephoning Poppy for a moan when her mum peered round the bedroom door.

"Can I come in?"

"If you're sure you can spare the time," Livi had replied sarcastically.

Her mum had sighed.

"I'm sorry I sounded off," she had said, perching on the end of Livi's bed. "I didn't mean it to come out like that—it's just that, well, that . . ." and to Livi's horror, her mother had burst into tears.

Livi had felt awful.

"It's OK, Mum," she had said, putting an arm round her shoulder. "I'm sorry—it was my fault."

Her mother shook her head. "No, it's me. I know I'm being irrational, but I am so tired and your father didn't send any money this month, and if I was thirty-five and slim like Rosalie, instead of forty-five with cellulite to spare, he might not have gone, and now the boiler is making funny noises again—and—oh everything!" she finished wearily.

"Dad'll be back," Livi had reassured her, more out of hope than conviction. "You're worth a thousand Rosalies," she added loyally.

"I don't think your father sees it that way," Livi's mum sniffed.

Livi tried again.

"Look, I'll make us some of that lemon and ginger tea you like, OK?"

Her mother gave her a watery smile and nodded.

"And you could nip down to the corner shop for doughnuts," she suggested, pulling a tissue from Livi's box and wiping her eyes.

"And we could get a weepy video," added Livi. "No, perhaps not a weepy one tonight . . ."

Livi's mum blew her nose and grinned.

"I'll get my purse," she said. And paused, her hand on the doorknob.

"You know, none of this would be so hard if I didn't still love your dad—even on the days when I hate him," she had added softly.

That, thought Livi, was the most promising confession her mother had made in weeks. She had given her an enormous hug and decided to work harder on her creative visualisation of Rosalie being squashed by a very fast moving vehicle. Soon, if possible.

"You know what your problem is?" said Hayley matter-of-factly, as the bus pulled up at their stop.

"I imagine you are going to tell me," said Livi, grabbing her bag from the overhead rack. Hayley was not known for her tact and diplomacy.

"You take it all too seriously," asserted Hayley. "Let them get on with sorting out their own lives and milk the situation for all it's worth."

She grinned at Livi's puzzled expression.

"Look, it's simple," she said, flicking her fringe out of her eyes. "They're wrapped up in their own problems, right? At the end of the day, they'll do whatever they're going to do regardless of what you think."

"It looks that way," admitted Livi as they pushed their way to the front of the bus.

"And I'll bet they are both eaten up with guilt—your dad because he was the one to leave, and your mum because she'll be doing the 'If only I'd been a better wife' bit."

"She was—is—a good wife," snapped Livi.

"That's not the point," said Hayley, jumping off the bus. "They all do the guilt thing any-way—it makes them feel better. My mum went on and on for ages about how if she had been less extravagant and spent more time keeping the house nice and doing Delia Smith recipes, Dad would have stayed and Damien wouldn't have fluffed his mocks. Then she met Clive and suddenly started getting her hair permed again and smothering herself in Dune, feeding us Tesco lasagne and not even noticing Damien's grades."

Livi giggled.

"Hey—it can laugh!" teased Hayley. "I thought the Doomsday look was fixed."

Livi pulled a face.

"So," continued Hayley determinedly, as they waited to cross the road. "What I'm saying is, you stop worrying about their lives and get one of your own! Use their guilt—I got my mum to agree to letting me have a party for my birthday next week, just because I came on strong about how I needed to forget the pain of the break-up!" She giggled.

"I even get to see Tim midweek, which used to be a total no-no! You have to make things work to your own advantage."

Livi sighed. Hayley, who never seemed to care whether she had a boyfriend or not, was going out with this guy of sixteen who worshipped the ground she walked on.

"Yes, well at least you've got someone else to be with," she said. "I haven't."

"You would have if only you'd just chill out a bit—I mean, look at the way you let Adam go!"

"What do you mean, I let him go?" bristled Livi. "He was the one who went swanning off."

"And have you asked yourself why?" countered Hayley, as they dodged the traffic on Wellington Road. "Boys aren't interested in hearing you going on and on about the Wretched Rachel—"

"Rosalie," corrected Livi.

"Rosalie, then," said Hayley impatiently. "The point is, guys like Adam are looking for a good laugh and—well, let's face it, you have been a bit gloomy lately."

Livi looked wounded.

"You never come to The Stomping Ground anymore," Hayley remarked. "Why not?"

Livi shrugged.

"Well, now that Poppy's not . . ."

"Oh, for heaven's sake, Livi!" snapped Hayley. "You're like a little kid—can't go anywhere unless someone's there to hold your hand. I mean, Poppy's great and all that, but you can't live your life in her shadow."

Livi bit her lip.

"Look," continued Hayley, grabbing her arm. "there's a gang of us going to The Stomping Ground on Saturday—do you want to come?"

"My dad might be coming down . . ." began Livi, switching her school bag from one shoulder to the other.

"There you go again!" exclaimed Hayley. "So your dad might come? But then again, on past record, he might not. What are you going to do—put your whole life on hold in case he deigns to call?"

"But . . ."

"But nothing. Come out with us on Saturday night—it'll be a blast."

Livi thought about it. Half of her wanted to go, to get in with the cool crowd and forget all the things that woke her up at two in the morning, but the other half was sure she wouldn't fit in, and that everyone would end up talking about her behind her back. It hadn't mattered when Poppy was around, because she always told Livi what to wear and who to chat up, but now . . .

"And if your dad does come, then he and your mum can have some time alone together," said Hayley craftily.

There is that, thought Livi. And a romantic evening, just the two of them, might do the trick.

"OK," she said. "I'll come—thanks."

"Cool," said Hayley. "See you!" She made to turn down Wellington Gardens.

"Do you want to come round to my house for a bit?" asked Livi hastily, partly out of gratitude and partly because she wanted company. "We could listen to my new Hang Out CD if you like."

Livi's greatest passion in the world was music—playing it, listening to it and even writing it when the mood took her—and she spent most of her allowance on CDs and sheet music.

"Better not," said Hayley, "I'm supposed to be helping Dad and Carole with the twins' birthday party. A dozen four-year-olds—manic! I'm only doing it because Dad said he'd get me that leather skirt from Togs if I kept Carole sweet."

Livi kicked an empty Coke can into the gutter.

"I envy you," she said. "It's like you've got two whole families—I'd love to have brothers or sisters."

Hayley pulled a face.

"You have to be joking!" she said. "There's never any peace anywhere; home is bedlam with my weirdo brother, Damien, playing the drums all the time and Clive's kids coming in and out whenever they've had a bust up with their mother—and in Dad's house you can't move without falling over dumper trucks or stepping on bits of Lego."

"Yes, but at least you never have time to feel lonely," observed Livi wistfully.

Hayley's face clouded for a moment.

"You do actually," she said. "See, my mum is so busy proving that she's this mega-cool stepmother and Dad is always rushing about kicking footballs, even though he's pushing fifty and has a paunch like a potato sack—and all the time, it's as if they don't bother about me because I've always been around." She paused. "You know, good old Hayley, she'll cope."

For a moment she stood, lost in thought, nibbling her thumbnail.

"So," she said, running her fingers through her caramel-coloured bob, and breaking into a broad grin again, "I just let them get on with it and do what I want. It's cool—try it!"

Livi grinned.

"I might," she said. "And thanks for the invitation."

"No probs," said Hayley. "There are some neat guys who go to the SG on a Saturday—you might find your dream date!"

"Boys never seem very interested in me," said Livi resignedly.

Hayley raised her eyebrows heavenwards.

"Stop being so negative!" she ordered. "You're mega pretty and nice with it, so stop putting yourself down all the time."

She grinned at her.

"For all you know, your whole life could change on Saturday night!"

There were times when Hayley Spicer appeared to have the gift of second sight.

enchanted encounter

After Hayley had scooted off to face two hours of pinning the tail on the Lion King, Livi wandered down Silverdale Road, trying to work out the best way to persuade her mother to cough up for some new gear for Saturday night. Her friends all seemed really clued up about style whereas Livi never felt she got it quite right. Of course, this was largely her mother's fault, because her allowance was so stingy that she could never get more than one thing at a time, and as Poppy said, you should always go for the total look. What she really wanted were some black lace hipsters and an angora top, but no way could she afford those right now.

Maybe, she thought with a sudden flash of inspiration, she should phone her father and feed him a tale of woe about being too ashamed to go out with her friends because she had nothing worth wearing. After all, if Hayley was to be believed, he would want to do all he could to keep Livi sweet. It might just be worth a try, if only because whatever her dad spent on her, he couldn't lavish on that conniving cow Rosalie.

The more she thought about it the more she liked the idea and broke into a run for the last hundred yards to her house, reciting her pathetic plea in her head. She was grappling with the rusting latch on the front gate when she felt a tap on her shoulder.

"Excuse me . . ."

She gasped out loud, wheeled round and found herself face to face with the most drop-dead gorgeous guy she had ever seen. He had almond-shaped grey eyes and hair the colour of peanut brittle, and was leaning on the handle-bars of a gleaming mountain bike. He was wearing an open-necked black sweatshirt and silver cycling shorts, which revealed a pair of gloriously muscular and sun-tanned legs. Livi reckoned he was about sixteen and as his gaze travelled from her windswept hair to her somewhat scuffed school shoes, she became very conscious of her shapeless uniform skirt and ghastly maroon blazer.

"I'm sorry," he said, "I didn't mean to scare you." His voice was deep and gravelly and had an extraordinary effect on Livi's heart rate.

"The thing is, I seem to be a bit lost," he said. "I'm trying to get back to Lockside Lane—you know, down by The Butty Inn?"

Livi nodded. It was halfway between her house and Canal End, where Poppy lived.

"That's easy," she said. "Just go to the bottom of this road, turn left into Watersmeet, and Lockside Lane is the last on the left. Which side of the canal do you want?"

"Haven't a clue!" he laughed. "I'm on a narrowboat and I left my mum looking for a mooring while I sussed out the neighbourhood. Knowing her boathandling skills, she could be halfway to Lowestoft by now!"

Livi laughed.

"Well, if you need to cross the canal, you'd do better to walk away from the pub up to the swing bridge and cross there," she said.

"Great—thanks a lot." He straddled his bike and wheeled round to face down the road.

"Have a nice holiday!" said Livi, surprising herself at her eagerness to continue the conversation.

"Oh, it's not a holiday," he said easily. "We're living on the boat all summer—it used to be moored further along at Kettleborough Locks but Mum's working round here for a bit and so here we are! I'm Ryan, by the way," he added with a grin.

"I'm Olivia," said Livi, reverting to her full name in the interests of sophistication.

"See you around, maybe?" said Ryan.

Yes please, thought Livi. When? Where?

Aloof and mysterious, she told herself firmly.

"Maybe," she said as casually as her pounding heart would let her.

She watched as he pedalled furiously down the road, raising one sun-tanned arm in a farewell wave.

This, thought Livi, acutely aware of the butterflies in her stomach and the total absence of her legs, must be what they mean by love at first sight.

rapturous
reunion

CHAPTER FOUR

Livi turned the key in the front door
and let herself into the hallway. A
large green pottery leprechaun leered
at her from the telephone table. Of the telephone there was no sign.

She grinned. Whenever her mum created a
new figure, she tried it out in the hall. If visi-
tors exclaimed in excitement about it, she
knew it was a hit. If they politely ignored it,
then it wouldn't sell and the idea was ditched.

Livi's mum saw her hallway as a sort of
showroom for her skills. When the Hunters
had first bought the house, it had been a narrow, gloomy passageway, but Judy had stripped
off the hideous red flock wallpaper, and rag
rolled the walls in lemon and cream, and
painted a tromp d'oeil of a window with doves
pecking at grains of corn on the wall. There

was a mirror framed with little fat fairies and a hat stand with goblins' faces for coat hooks. A candle holder shaped like a man in the moon sat on the table, and at the foot of the stairs were a pair of terracotta elves, one picking his nose and the other sucking his thumb. From the ceiling hung some Peruvian wind chimes, a cluster of shimmering crystals, which Judy swore would bring creative energy into the house, and a bronze incense burner that she had unearthed in a junk shop. The overall effect was somewhat eccentric, and Poppy's mother had declared that the Edwardian builder would be turning in his grave; but as Livi's mum said, he didn't have to live there and at least the conversations it engendered were a lot more interesting than talking about the weather.

Livi hurled her blazer over one of the goblin faces, went through to the den and sank down in front of the piano. She started playing. Ryan. Ryan. She repeated the name like a mantra in her head. Now, he was the sort of guy she could really fancy. Someone mature and easy to talk to—and that body! She wished she'd thought to ask the name of the boat; the Leehampton Canal was crowded with barges and narrowboats all summer and she doubted she'd ever see him again. Unless, of course, she got Poppy onto the case . . .

That was brilliant! Poppy's cottage fronted the towpath; it was perfect. She would get Poppy to scan all the boats till she found Ryan and then report back to Livi. Then Livi could just happen to be passing, dressed to kill, and everything would be great.

The thought of the cash necessary to dress even halfway to kill reminded Livi of her resolve to phone her dad. She hunted around among the coats and magazines and craft shop samples and assorted boots and shoes that dotted the hallway and eventually found the telephone under a copy of the *Leehampton Echo*. She dialled her father's number and prayed that the dreaded Rosalie wouldn't answer.

"Livi! Angel! How are you?"

"Fine," began Livi. And then realised that she was still getting the ringing tone and no one had answered the phone.

She swung round. Standing behind her, his sandy hair all awry, and with a great grin spreading from ear to ear, was her father.

"Dad! Dad!" Livi dropped the receiver and found herself enveloped in a bear-like hug. She took a deep breath savouring the smell of him, sandalwood aftershave with a hint of the pear drops he always sucked in the car. She felt tears pricking behind her eyes and realised that she had missed him even more than she knew.

"Surprised to see me?"

Livi nodded, still grinning.

"Well, you'll be even more surprised when you hear my news." He held her at arm's length and looked her up and down. "You're looking prettier than ever, Livi—breaking guys' hearts right, left, and centre, I shouldn't wonder."

I wish, thought Livi.

"What news?" she asked eagerly, following him through to the kitchen. Perhaps Rosalie had thrown him out and he was coming home to live for ever. "What is it, Dad?"

Her dad held up a hand. "No, not yet—wait till your mum gets back."

"She's not here?" Livi looked puzzled. "So how did you get in?"

Her dad put his hand in his trouser pocket and waved a key.

"I've still got a door key," he said. "After all, it's still partly my house." He opened the tea caddie and put two tea bags into the pot. It made Livi feel wonderfully comfortable to see him doing everyday things in the house in the way he used to.

"Do you know when she will be back?" Mike asked, rather anxiously, it seemed to Livi.

"Hang on," said Livi. "She usually leaves a note."

She ran back up the hall and looked underneath the thumb-sucking pixie, and sure enough there was a Post-it note covered in her mother's slanting scrawl.

Dear Livi,   4:30 PM
  Have gone to see Mrs. Liddington about a goblin jardiniere to go with her umbrella stand. Back about six—can you put something from the freezer into the oven? Choose what you

like. And could you bring the washing in?
Thanks.

Love, Mum

P.S. Some boy phoned. Didn't catch the
name.

Oh great, thought Livi. She can remember all
the chores I have to do, but writing down one
name is too much for her. Perhaps it was Adam,
phoning to confess that Abigail just wasn't right
for him, and it was Livi all along. But somehow,
when she thought of Adam, all she saw was
Ryan's sun-tanned cheeks and gorgeous eyes.
And besides, for now not even that mattered.
Dad was here.

From the kitchen came a boisterous rendi-
tion of "Blue Suede Shoes." Mike Hunter's
musical prowess was yet another attribute he
had passed on to his daughter, but unlike Livi,
who sailed through piano and oboe exams with
the greatest of ease but hated performing in
public, Mike's exuberance and love of the lime-
light reflected itself in a passion for playing the
electric guitar and singing fifties and sixties

rock, his specialty being his Elvis impression, which Livi found inordinately embarrassing, especially when he did it within earshot of any of her friends.

"Mah bloooo-oo sue-ah . . ." Livi grinned and pushed open the kitchen door.

"She'll be back at six," she announced.

Mike stopped in mid flourish with the tea towel and glanced at his watch.

"You are going to stay for supper, aren't you, Dad?" she added, ferreting in the freezer for something to cook.

"Well, I don't know." Her father sounded hesitant.

"Oh, please," pleaded Livi. "You haven't been down for ages," she added accusingly.

Mike looked uncomfortable and stirred the teapot.

"I ought to get on—there's so much to do with the move and . . ."

He stopped.

Livi stood up, a packet of frozen moussaka in one hand.

"Move?" she said.

Her father clamped his hands to his head in mock horror.

"There I go, letting the cat out of the bag," he said. "Oh well, I might as well tell you now—we can fill Mum in on it all when she gets back. Sit down, love."

Livi hurled the moussaka back into the freezer and pulled up a chair.

"What would you say if I told you that I was moving back to Leehampton?"

Livi let out a squeal of delight.

"Oh Dad, that's wonderful!" She jumped up and hugged him. "Oh, I've prayed and prayed that you would!"

Her father grinned.

"It'll be great, won't it?" he said, unbuttoning his cuffs and rolling up the sleeves of his shirt. "I've missed you so much and now there will be no more rushing up and down motorways whenever I want to see you."

The thought struck Livi that there hadn't been much rushing in evidence. She dismissed such disloyalty immediately. Dad was coming home because he missed them and that was all that mattered.

"Brilliant!" Livi thought she would burst with happiness.

"But what about your job?" she added hastily, remembering that a large number of the earlier rows had centred around her father's tendency to change employment with the frequency that most men changed their socks.

"Well," said her father examining the pattern on the tablecloth in some detail, "I was never really suited for that post with Tough Toys, you know." He paused. "They made some voluntary redundancies and I offered—give me a chance to branch out into pastures new," he added ebulliently. "And of course, to be with you."

"So you're out of work?" Livi thought it best not to mince words.

"Temporarily," admitted her father, getting up to pour out the tea. "But of course, being back down here, close to all my old colleagues, I shall find something much more suitable in a flash." He snapped his fingers to emphasise the antici- pated ease of this job-finding exercise.

Livi had one nasty moment imagining her

mother's face when she discovered that on the one hand, Mike was coming home and on the other, he didn't have any work. She did hope Mum wouldn't make a scene about it; the great thing was that Mum and Dad would be back together again and everything could return to normal. She was so excited that she didn't know whether to laugh or to cry.

"When are you moving back?" asked Livi. Now that the decision had been made she wanted him away from the clutches of the Wretched Rosalie as soon as possible.

"You could move in tonight—your den is still like it was, except that mum has two dozen varnished fairies drying in there." She giggled.

"She can move those, though," she added hastily, not wanting her father to think that his space had been taken over.

Mike looked puzzled.

"I hardly think that your mum would want me and Rosalie to . . . oh, Livi, you didn't think I meant I was moving back *here, to this house*, did you?"

Livi swallowed. That was precisely what she

had thought. Dad, back here, where he should be. She didn't trust herself to speak. She felt as if all the bounce and happiness and excitement of two minutes ago was draining away through her feet.

"No, sweetheart—we're both coming down. We've found a nice house to rent and we move in tomorrow. Neither of us wanted to live in Runcorn long term."

He eyed her stricken expression. "Well, I don't suppose anyone *wants* to live in Runcorn long term," he laughed, in an attempt to bring a smile to her face.

Livi bit her lip and turned away. Long term. That sounded as if Dad had no intention of ever coming back home. Long term sounded final. Livi's throat closed up and she felt sick. How could he?

"You shouldn't be anywhere with *her* long term!" she shouted. "You should be here! Mum's still your wife, for God's sake, and if you really loved me, you'd be here all the time not shacking up with some worthless bimbo!"

"Livi!" Mike stood up, a flush spreading over his face. "Don't speak about Rosalie like that!

43 ❋

After all, it's because of her . . ."

"I'll speak about Rosalie however I like!" shouted Livi. "I hate her! I wish she was dead!"

And with that she burst into tears. Her father pushed back his chair, walked over to her and wrapped her in his arms but she pushed him away.

"Don't!" she shouted, her disappointment erupting in a great flood of anger. "You don't mean it! You don't love me!"

"I do, Livi, I do, you have to believe me," pleaded her father, running his fingers through his hair. "Look, please, just listen for a minute. There's more. What's happened is that Rosalie has . . ."

"Why should I listen? I don't want to hear about anything to do with that hateful woman!" Livi brushed away a tear from her cheek.

"I know it's been hard for you, sweetheart, but which would you rather have? Me and Rosalie down here, where you and I can get to do things together and have fun, or me and Rosalie two hundred miles away when all we get is a few hours on a Sunday once a month?"

Livi said nothing. What she really wanted was her dad, here with them, all the time, and Rosalie nowhere on the entire planet. She wanted her father back home where he belonged, but she was beginning to realise with sickening certainty that that wasn't an option.

"Livi?"

She looked at him. A frown puckered his brow, and he had the same expression on his face that he used to wear when he got home late from the pub for Sunday lunch and her mum was in a mood. She was so angry with him. She hated what he was doing to them both. But she loved him so much that it hurt.

"I want to see as much of you as I can," she confessed.

Her father's shoulders visibly relaxed and he smiled gently at her.

"So let's look forward to that, shall we? Once you get to know Rosalie better, you'll like her. I know you will."

Fat chance, thought Livi, but said nothing. She fiddled with the corner of the tablecloth. It would be nice to have Dad nearby though—and of course, if Mum played her cards right, she would be in a far better position to prove to him that he would be much happier living with them. Livi brightened somewhat at the thought. She would really have to take her mother in hand and get her to see that she must start presenting herself as the embodiment of what Clarissa Carradine called female mystique.

"Does Mum know?" she asked her father.

"Does Mum know what?" Judy Hunter appeared at the doorway carrying two loaded carrier bags and looking very flushed.

She glanced at Mike, coloured, smiled nervously and took a deep breath.

"Hi, Mike. What are you doing here?" she asked.

"Hi, Judy," said Mike, standing up and giving her a peck on the cheek. He shuffled uneasily. "You're looking well."

He still fancies her, thought Livi with an upsurge of hope. Judy said nothing. She was eyeing Livi's flushed face and bright eyes suspiciously.

"Any more tea in the pot, Livi? That

※ 46

Liddington woman is enough to try the patience of a saint."

Livi grabbed the pot and began pouring, although she had a feeling her mother would need something stronger than a cup of tea by the time Dad had finished.

Mike cleared his throat nervously.

"I happened to be in the area and I—I just popped in to give Livi some news."

Livi watched him. He seemed somehow less at ease, more diminished now her mother was in the room. Which was odd when you considered that Dad was nearly six foot and built like a rugby player and Mum was five foot four and looked as if a mild breeze would blow her away.

"Oh yes?" said Judy enquiringly.

"I'm moving back to Leehampton," said Mike in a rush.

Livi saw her mother's eyes widen and brighten.

"With Rosalie," Mike added.

Slowly, Judy's eyes dropped and the eagerness left her face. It was then that Livi discovered that feeling someone else's pain was as bad as hurting yourself.

"New job?" asked her mother in resigned tones.

"Well, no, actually, I took voluntary redundancy—never suited me that job—my expertise is in an altogether different field . . ."

"So you're out of work." It wasn't a question.

"Well, yes, but I have lots of irons in the fire and the pay is much better down here," Mike gabbled. "And the redundancy money wasn't bad—I'll be able to give you part of it," he added eagerly, rather like a small boy hoping that news of his new paper round would take people's minds off the broken kitchen window.

"Thanks," said Livi's mum dully. "That would help." She busied herself unpacking shopping onto the counter top.

There was an uncomfortable silence.

"Well, I'll be off," said Mike eventually. "Look, Livi, how about I take you out to lunch on Saturday?"

Livi chewed her lip. She wanted to spend some more time with her father, if only to get him to see the error of his ways, but she could see how upset her mum was. She looked at her mother's rigid back and felt the sympathy give way to anger. Why didn't she do something, say something, shout, argue, anything to try to prove to Dad how much she loved him. But instead she was silently and methodically stacking tins of curried beans in the kitchen cupboard. Dad would think she didn't even care.

"Mum?"

Her mother spoke without turning round.

"I shall be at Kettleborough Craft Fair all day on Saturday, so you go and have a good time," she said flatly.

Livi looked at her dad, leaning uneasily against the Welsh dresser waiting for a reply. She thought about Hayley and how she said that when parents were treating you like this, you should milk the situation for all it was worth.

"OK, I'll come," said Livi, as casually as she could. "But I'll need you to drop me home by five, okay?"

"Can't see why not," said her father, pleased to have the conversation on a more mundane level. "Got a date, have you?" he said, giving her a nudge and a knowing wink.

"I'm going out with my mates in the evening," she said, rather liking how the words made her sound one of the gang.

"I didn't know that," said her mother in surprise.

"Well, you do now," said Livi, and immediately hated herself for taking all her disappointment and anger out on her mum.

"Olivia! I'll thank you not to take that tone of voice," said Judy sharply.

"Livi! You shouldn't speak to your mum like that!" expostulated her father at the same time.

Oh great, thought Livi. You two are at loggerheads for weeks on end, but you can still manage to see eye to eye when it comes to nagging me. Neither of you give a toss for how I feel inside.

Then she remembered Hayley's ruse for getting her own way.

"Sorry, mum," she said meekly, looking up from underneath her long lashes. "It's just . . ." she faltered . . . "I'm so confused."

Her mother shot her a knowing glance, but her father laid a hand on her shoulder.

"I know, sweetheart, I do understand how you feel."

Like hell you do, thought Livi.

"Hayley's invited me out to The Stomping Ground on Saturday evening," she said wistfully. "But I might not go."

"Why not? You'll enjoy it—isn't that the hip place in town?" said her father, who always tried to sound young and clued up.

"It is if you've got the gear, which I haven't," she said sadly. "I don't suppose, Dad, you could possibly let me have some money?"

Mike looked at Judy, who began paying minute attention to the contents of the fridge.

"I don't see why not," he said, producing his wallet from his back pocket. "It's time your old dad treated you, isn't it?"

Livi took the outstretched £20 note.

Yes, she thought coldly, it is.

"Thanks, Dad—you're a star," she said with what she hoped was a winning smile.

livi makes her feelings known

After Livi had waved goodbye to her father, whose battered old Granada clanked its way up Silverdale Road in a cloud of exhaust fumes, she went back into the kitchen, resolving to be nice to her mother.

She found her sitting at the kitchen table with her head in her hands.

"Mum . . ." she began tentatively, putting an arm on her shoulder.

Judy sprang to her feet, and glared at Livi. There was a smudge of mascara below her right eye and her nose looked pink.

"I specifically asked you to put something in the oven for supper—where is it?"

Oh sugar, thought Livi. Bad move.

"Sorry. I forgot," she said. "I was talking to Dad and . . ."

"Oh yes? Well, that would explain it, wouldn't it?" snapped her mother, opening the freezer and rummaging through the shelves. "After all, chatting to your father is far more enthralling than doing anything whatever to help me! Never mind that I've been sucking up to that ghastly Liddington woman for the last two hours, listening to her outlandish ideas on interior design, all so that I could get one more measly commission and pay the council tax. Never mind that I am exhausted and wanted to sit down and not have to worry about food and . . ."

"Sorry, I'll do us some . . ." Livi began appeasingly.

But Judy was in full flood and not about to be restrained.

"And the washing? Did you bring that in? Of course you didn't because Dad was here and you forgot. Nothing in life is as important as Dad, is it?"

Livi stopped trying to be conciliatory.

"No!" she shouted, forgetting that she was

miffed with her father and leaping to his defence. "No, right now it's not! You didn't even try, did you? You could have been really nice to him, and made a fuss of him, and then he'd have thought twice about staying with the Wretched Rosalie—but you couldn't be bothered, could you? You tell me you love him, but you never tell him. I don't believe a word of it!"

Judy opened her mouth to speak but Livi didn't give her the chance.

"Dad's going to be living back here in Leehampton, and you'll have your best chance ever of getting him back and all you're worried about is some stupid washing! Aren't you even a bit pleased?"

Judy ran a hand wearily over her forehead.

"For you? Yes of course. I know how much you have missed Dad and it will be good for you to have him nearby. But for me? No. No, I'm not pleased."

She bit her lip and swallowed.

"I'm not pleased that every day I will run the risk of bumping into Rosalie in the High Street, or seeing the two of them driving round town.

I'm not pleased that the man I love is crass enough to bring his—his mistress to live on our doorstep."

She sighed.

"I suppose in the end it boils down to one thing. I'm not pleased that she has got him and I haven't."

Her mother looked suspiciously close to tears and Livi began to feel badly about having yelled so much. She hadn't thought about the risks of her mum bumping into Rosalie. She took her mother's hand.

"Then fight to get him back," she urged, more gently. "That's what you have to do—not just take it all lying down. You should have told him you loved him, you should have begged him to come back. You should have promised that things would be different from now on. You didn't even make it sound like you cared," she added accusingly.

Judy said nothing.

"From now on, Mum, you really have to work on him," Livi went on emphatically. "Make him feel like he is the most important person in the whole world, find excuses to call him up, make sure that you always have that walnut cake he likes ready when he comes round . . ."

Her mother held up a weary hand.

"Livi, I know you mean well, honestly I do— and I know that you can't possibly understand all the implications—but will you do just one thing for me?"

"What?" asked Livi sulkily, assuming that she was about to get lumbered with making omelettes for supper yet again.

"Allow me a little dignity," said Judy and got up and walked out of the room.

Livi went through to the piano, sat down, and began strumming out a lilting Irish folk dance. But she couldn't concentrate. She kept thinking about the situation.

And still couldn't understand either of her parents.

problems, problems

Livi had little time the following day to brood on the shortcomings of either of her parents because too many other considerations fought for her attention. She had phoned Poppy before she left for school and recounted the story of meeting the amazing Ryan and the pressing need for his whereabouts to be discovered and noted. Poppy, who enjoyed a challenge, promised she would keep an eye open along the towpath, but decided that she needed an exact description and a detailed strategy and suggested meeting Livi after school to work it all out. This cheered Livi enormously; with Poppy on the case, another meeting with Ryan was as good as sorted.

Her mind was further occupied because it was her turn to play the piano for the Year

Nine Assembly, which meant she had to get up half an hour earlier than usual to practise, and then couldn't eat her breakfast because a squadron of butterflies was looping the loop in her stomach. It didn't matter that she could have played any number of hymns with her eyes shut and one hand tied behind her back; the thought of sitting up on the platform with all those eyes looking at her made her feel horribly sick. Once she got started, the music carried her along and it was as if there was no one else in the room; but thinking about it beforehand quite put her off her muesli. Each week, she tried to get out of it, but Gee-Gee said that learning performance skills was an integral part of social development, which was headmasterspeak for, "You play and Miss Sterry can have the morning off to take her mother to the doctor."

After the usual end-of-week pep talk from Gee-Gee about playing hard at the weekend in order to be ready to work hard on Monday, and a couple of notices about lost hockey sticks and kindly not sticking chewing gum on the Art Room windowsill, the headmaster took a deep breath and beamed beatifically at the assembled throng.

"And now," he said, "I have some most exciting news."

This did not evoke any reaction from his audience, because the headmaster's idea of excitement was usually the installation of a new fire alarm or the impending visit of some dry-as-dust school governor.

"As you know, we are rapidly approaching the school's bi-centenary—that's 200 years to the non-mathematical among us," he joked. "And to celebrate this momentous occasion we will be holding a Gala Weekend."

"Oh whoopee!" muttered an ill-advised pupil and received a black look and a request to attend the head's study after Assembly.

"Your class tutors will fill you in on the various plans—art displays, a special edition of the Bellborough magazine and so forth—but there is one rather special aspect of our history that I am most keen to have included."

A number of bottoms shuffled in boredom on the hard floor, and a couple of paper darts took a brief flight over the Swiss cheese plant at the foot of the podium.

Mr. Golding fixed the culprits with the sort of stare that paralyses wildlife at twenty paces and continued.

"You will know that our founder, Sir Ambrose Bellborough, had the idea of setting up a school for orphans and the children of poor families who would otherwise receive no education."

He made a pyramid of his fingers and touched the tip of his nose in a gesture which, Livi thought, seemed universal to all academics trying to think what to say next.

"To ignore this aspect of our history as part of our Gala Weekend celebrations would be to deny the great philanthropic role Sir Ambrose played in the establishment of our school."

More bottom shuffling, this time accompanied by coughs, whispers and a retinue of watch alarms all going off at once.

"And so," declared Gee-Gee, "as the centre-piece to our evening concert on Gala Day, in which the entire school will participate, I am asking Year Nine to produce a portrayal in words and music of the beginnings of Bellborough Court School, from its inception in the attic room of that factory in Leehampton to its removal to this"—Gee-Gee paused and waved an expansive arm around the hall—"the one-time country home of the Bellboroughs of Leehampton."

Mr. Golding closed his eyes momentarily as if savouring the magnificence of his words, and a low buzz went round the back of the room, a mixture of groans from those who thought the whole idea totally naff, and enthusiasm from the handful of hopeful Keanu Reeveses and Kate Winslets.

Gee-Gee tapped the lectern with his hand.

"I am asking our two Year Nine music scholars, Luke Cunningham and Olivia Hunter, to take responsibility for that. With a little guidance from the music staff, of course," he concluded.

Livi, who had been contemplating the state of her fingernails during Gee-Gee's ramblings, jumped at the sound of her name and a few people laughed. She felt her cheeks burning and started flicking over her sheets of music in an attempt to look nonchalant.

"And now, Olivia, the recessionary music, if you please," requested Mr. Golding.

Livi grabbed the music and it shot all over the floor. More laughter.

By the time she had collected the wayward sheets and begun playing Sea Shanty number four her hands were shaking and she wanted the floor to open and swallow her up. She made five mistakes in the first eleven bars, something she had never done before.

She couldn't do it. She wasn't the organising sort. Come to think of it, neither was Luke. He was a brill musician but it took him ten minutes to choose between soup and salad at lunchtime. Mr. Golding had obviously made a complete mess up here. She'd have to tell him. He would have to get someone else.

As she crossed the yard to put her music away in the locker room, she found half her class clustered around Abigail Lane, who was fingering a silver necklace and looking enormously smug.

"Hi, Livi!" she purred. "I was just showing these guys what Adam bought me." She tilted her chin and smiled at Livi in a challenging sort of way. "It's a love token," she added triumphantly.

Livi felt herself blush. Most of Year Nine knew how crazy she had been about Adam, and she was certain that they were all waiting to see her reaction.

"That's nice," she muttered, thinking miserably that all Adam had ever bought *her* was a bag of popcorn when they went to the cinema.

"Isn't it just?" crowed Abigail, scooping up a handful of chestnut hair, twisting it into a knot and sticking a wooden barrette through it. This had the immediate effect of both showing off her slender neck and the much prized necklace and making Livi feel even more envious than she had done before. Abby was everything that Livi aspired to be and knew she wasn't. She was not only blessed with stunning looks and a model figure but had stacks of confidence and never seemed to feel embarrassed or unsure. What Abby Lane wanted, Abby Lane got. She'd never taken much notice of Livi before, but now she was with Adam she seemed to want to remind her of the fact at every possible moment.

"That must have cost a fortune," breathed Hayley, stroking the chain.

Abby grinned.

"I guess Adam reckons I'm worth it," she said with a toss of her head. "I suppose," she added, throwing a pointed glance at Livi, "he's enjoying having a girlfriend who knows how to have a good time. Unlike some people I could mention."

And, with a toss of her head and a smug smile, she sauntered off.

"Take no notice," whispered Hayley. "It won't last—you know Adam. He'll have found someone else to impress with his charms by next week."

Adam was not renowned for his unswerving loyalty.

"You don't suppose she and Adam . . ." began Livi.

"'Course not," asserted Hayley. "Even Abby's not that stupid. She's all talk."

All talk or not, thought Livi, she's the one with Adam.

tears and temptations

The bell was already ringing for first period as Livi ran into the locker room to put her music away. It was French, which she hated and could see little point in, since every French person she had ever met spoke perfectly serviceable English. Livi preferred logical subjects like math and science, that had rules that made sense and never changed. Worse still, it was Friday, so it would be reading comprehension, which meant concentrating like crazy, and how could she be expected to concentrate with the thought of this concert hanging over her head?

She was just picking up *Allez en France* when she heard the sound of sniffing.

She turned and saw Adam's twin sister, Tasha, sitting at the far corner of the room, knees hunched up to her chin, sobbing quietly into a crumpled tissue.

"Hey, Tasha, what's wrong?" Livi went over and sat down beside her and put an arm round her shoulder.

"Nothing!" Tasha jumped to her feet and brushed Livi's arm away. "Nothing's wrong—leave me alone!"

"Sorry!" Livi felt wounded. "I was only trying to help."

Tasha gulped. She was tiny for her age and looked more like twelve than fourteen. She had huge black deep-set eyes, olive skin, and a head of tight black curls. Her heart-shaped face was streaked with tears. Not only was she much darker than her twin brother, but she was the complete opposite to him in almost every way. While Adam flirted outrageously and was always cracking jokes and bragging about how he'd ducked out of homework yet again, Tasha was very quiet and timid and hadn't made any close friends.

"It's OK, I'm just having a bad day." She tried a lopsided smile. "It's nothing, honestly. I'd better get off to French."

Livi remembered something Mrs. Joll had told Poppy when Adam and Tasha had started at Bellborough in the middle of last term. She had said, in the way that teachers do when they want you to be nice to someone but not ask questions, that the twins had had "some problems" and might need help. It occurred to Livi that no one knew much about the Reillys—they never invited anyone back to the house they shared with their grandparents, and even when Livi had been going out with Adam, he never talked about his family. Maybe Tasha was having as much trouble with parents as Livi experienced with hers.

They walked up the corridor together, Tasha rubbing fiercely at her eyes in an attempt to remove all trace of tears.

"You are sure there's nothing I can do?" Livi asked. She knew what it was like to feel miserable; at least when she had gone through a bad patch last term she had had Poppy to sort her out. Tasha didn't appear to have anyone.

"Shall I get Adam?" offered Livi. "He's in my French set."

"No way!" Tasha was adamant. "And please, don't tell him you saw me crying, all right? Promise!" she asked urgently.

"Promise," said Livi. "If that's what you want."

"It is," affirmed Tasha. "It really is."

During the morning, Livi found herself repeatedly thinking about Tasha. She had a feeling that something big had upset her, but she didn't know what to do about it. Of course, if Poppy had been here, she would have known exactly the right things to say and do to get Tasha to open up. But Poppy wasn't here. Maybe she could enlist the help of someone else.

"Have you seen Tasha?" she asked Hayley over lunch.

Hayley, who was demolishing a wedge of pizza at something approaching the speed of light, shook her head, her mouth being too full of pepperoni to allow for speech in any form.

"What do you want her for?" asked Tamsin, spooning banana yoghurt into her mouth. "Right little wimp she is."

Tamsin was inclined to think that anyone who couldn't play the lead in *The Tempest*, win the athletics cup two years running, and remove spiders from the washbasins without flinching, was a total no-hoper.

"She's not," protested Livi, "she's just—shy, I suppose."

"Pathetic, more like," said Abigail dismissively, fiddling with her locket and sipping a Diet Tango. "She's such a mouse. How come she can be so different from Adam?"

"Hey, what about this concert then?" said Tamsin. "I fancy myself in one of those Jane Austen dresses, reclining on a chaise longue."

"And I could be an emaciated pauper!" giggled Hayley, sinking her teeth into a custard tart.

"With hips like yours?" sneered Abigail. "Hardly."

Hayley blushed and said nothing. Livi resisted the urge to wring Abby's neck.

"And Livi will be penning heartrending lyrics about poverty-stricken orphans scratching away with quill pens!" quipped Mia, noticing

Hayley's discomfort. "That right, Livi?"

Livi shook her head.

"I'm telling Gee-Gee I can't do it," she said. "It's crazy—I am useless at all that stuff."

"You play brilliantly," protested Hayley. "Half the time, you don't even need music."

"Playing's one thing—organising a whole concert is something else," said Livi. "No way."

No one said a word. They knew from experience that Mr. Golding was not one to be easily swayed.

Tamsin pushed her empty yoghurt carton to one side and peeled an orange.

"Livi, Hayley says you're coming to The Stomping Ground tomorrow," she said, deliberately changing the subject and making it sound as if Livi's appearance at such a hip venue equated with the Queen turning up at the fish counter in Safeways.

Livi nodded.

"Brill!" said Tamsin doubtfully. "What are you wearing?"

Livi tried to sound casual.

"Oh, I haven't really decided yet," she said,

hoping it would seem as if her wardrobe was so jammed full of great gear that the only problem was one of choice. She made a mental note to take her £20 to Togs 'n' Clogs first thing in the morning.

"I've got this amazing new lace dress," said Abby. "Shoestring straps and a plunge neckline—that'll wow them down the SG!"

Livi's heart sank.

"Are Abby and Adam really going?" she asked Hayley as Abby took her tin to the recycling bin.

" 'Course," said Hayley. "Where else is there worth going in Leehampton on a Saturday night if you're not eighteen?"

Livi bit her lip.

"Maybe I'll give it a miss this time," she ventured.

"What? And let Abby 'I love myself to pieces' Lane think you can't stand the competition! No way!"

Livi was hesitating as Abby swanned back.

"You're not with anyone right now, are you, Livi?" she said, offering a fake sympathetic smile.

Oh, go drown in a vat of oil, thought Livi.

"Actually, there is this guy I met," she said casually.

"Really?" Tamsin interjected. "What's he like? Where did you meet him?" Tamsin always came to life at the mention of anything male.

"You never said," muttered Hayley, who really did like to be first with every piece of news.

"You'll meet him soon enough," said Livi, her heart thumping in her chest as she realised just how deep she was digging herself in.

"Why don't you bring him along to the disco?" purred Abby, picking up her books. "Then we can all give him the once over. If," she added, throwing a narrowed glance at Livi, "he actually exists."

As they changed for PE, Hayley pumped Livi for information.

"You're a dark horse—what's with this guy?" she said.

"Oh, it's nothing," confessed Livi. "Just some boy I got chatting to outside my house. But Abby goes on and on, and she is so patronising."

She paused and thought just how Abigail would gloat when she turned up without the mythical boyfriend.

"Maybe I won't come on Saturday after all," she ventured again.

"You're coming!" said Hayley firmly. "You'll enjoy it—you'll be surprised."

Which as it turned out was a somewhat prophetic remark.

gee-gee has the last word

At the end of the afternoon, Livi tapped on Mr. Golding's study door. She had rehearsed over and over in her head precisely what she was going to say to him and was sure that he would see things from her point of view.

"Olivia! Come in!" Mr. Golding waved her towards an armchair. "What can I do for you?"

"It's about this concert you want me to get involved in . . ." she began.

"Terrific, terrific, that's what I like to see— someone so keen they want to get started right away."

Livi cleared her throat.

"Well, not really, sir, you see . . ."

"Of course," interrupted Gee-Gee, "we

shouldn't be having this discussion without Luke—wouldn't want him to feel left out, would we?"

"No sir, but you see what I am trying to say is I can't possibly do it."

Gee-Gee looked as amazed as if Livi had informed him that she had forgotten her three times table.

"Can't *do* it?" He leaned back in his chair and frowned. "Of course you can do it. My goodness, you're one of our leading music scholars. And Mr. Ostler says that your oboe playing is coming along most splendidly."

"But that's just playing, sir," protested Livi, wondering why it took someone who was supposed to have been the toast of Oxford so long to catch on to a simple truth. "I can't produce this gala thing."

"Why not? When have you produced them in the past?" asked the head.

"Never, sir—that's the whole point; it's not my thing," declared Livi. "I'm not a good organiser."

"Well, my dear, if you have never tried it, how

do you know you cannot do it? I rather think you will surprise yourself. Now was there anything else?"

"You mean you're not going to find someone else to take my place?" asked Livi incredulously. "You have to!"

Mr. Golding inclined his head and smiled.

"I don't have to do anything of the sort, Olivia. After all, why should I when I am certain I have found the right person?"

Livi decided to try one more time.

"But sir, what if I mess up totally? What if the whole thing is a complete flop?"

Mr. Golding shrugged his shoulders.

"Then I shall have been proved wrong in my judgement, won't I?" he said.

Livi gave up and turned to the door.

"And Olivia . . ." he added.

Livi turned.

"If it is any comfort to you, I am very rarely proved wrong," he said with a twinkle in his eye.

As she shut Mr. Golding's door behind her, resisting with some difficulty the desire to slam it very loudly, she saw Luke Cunningham hurrying towards her.

"Hi, Livi," he said, pushing his glasses up the bridge of his nose and looking worried. "Look, no offence to you or anything, but I'm going to tell old Golding that no way can I get involved in this concert thing."

"Luke . . ." began Livi.

"No Livi, I'm sorry, don't try to persuade me," gabbled Luke. "I mean, I'll play and everything to support you. I'll transpose music, I'll even compose stuff, but I am sorry, I just don't have organisational skills. I shall just go in there and give it to him straight."

Livi looked at him with a wry grin on her face.

"I wish you luck," she said. "Are you good at coping with disappointment?"

judy makes a move

Poppy was waiting for Livi on the corner of Silverdale Road.

"So who's this guy?" she demanded, after hugging Livi enthusiastically. "Tell me everything."

"There isn't much to tell, really," admitted Livi, "except that he's spending the summer on a narrowboat with his mum and he has these incredible legs and he's just so amazing!"

Poppy laughed.

"Great description—good thing he's not wanted by Interpol. There must be a thousand boys like that," she said.

Livi shook her head.

"Not like him—he is something else," she insisted. "I've never met anyone like him."

"Except Ben and Todd and Adam . . ." grinned Poppy.

CHAPTER NINE

Livi pulled a face at her.

"Come in and I'll tell you all I know. And I've got loads of other stuff to fill you in on. Watch out for the leprechaun," she warned, ramming her key into the lock.

She pushed open the door and stopped dead. The hallway was full of furniture—chairs, coffee table, magazine racks. Livi realised that half of it was the contents of her father's den.

"What's going on?" she muttered. "Mum! Mu-um!"

There was a clattering and a muffled swearing and her mother emerged from the cellar, her forehead smudged with dirt and a small cobweb entwined in her hair.

"Oh, there you are," she panted. "Hello, Poppy dear. I won't kiss you—I'm a bit mucky."

"Hi, Mrs. Hunter—I like the leprechaun!" said Poppy, who had been brought up to observe the social niceties.

"Really? Oh, I am glad," enthused Judy. "I have a great affection for him but you never know how these things will go down. I shall make another one and try to sell him."

79

She flicked her hair out of her face and succeeded in smearing green paint over her forehead.

Livi eyed her with some distaste.

"Mum, what are you *doing?*" she asked.

"Reorganising," declared her mother briskly. "I'm moving all my work stuff out of the back bedroom."

Livi frowned.

"Why? That's your workshop."

"Not anymore," said her mother. "I'm turning it back into a bedroom. I've decided to take a lodger."

If her mother had announced her intention to join an enclosed order of silent, teetotal nuns, Livi could not have been more amazed.

"A *lodger?*" Livi spat out the word.

"Great idea, isn't it?" said her mum, choosing to ignore the implied criticism in her daughter's voice. "Don't you think so, Poppy?"

"You can't take a lodger!" expostulated Livi, preventing a thankful Poppy from having to reply.

"It'll help pay the bills which is more to the point," stressed her mother.

"But Dad said he was going to give you some money," Livi reminded her, anxious to keep memories of her father's generosity alive in her mother's mind. "And besides," she added, "I don't want a stranger living in my house. And where will you work?"

"In the den, of course—that's why I'm dragging all this junk of your father's down into the cellar. You two could help me if you like," she added, although in a tone that suggested she held out little hope of the offer being accepted.

"You are doing what?" Livi exploded. "You have no right to do that—that's Dad's stuff! What if he decides to come back? Which he will, sooner or later. What will he think—that you don't even care enough to look after his things? She can't do that, can she Poppy?"

Poppy looked embarrassed. For one thing, she hardly felt it was any of her business what Mrs. Hunter did in her own house, and for another, she had known Livi's mum for long enough to be perfectly aware that she would not be influenced by the opinions of two fourteen-year-olds, however well informed they might be.

Judy took a deep breath and fixed a smile on her face.

"I cannot put my whole life on hold while your father makes up his mind about what to do with his," she declared. It occurred to Livi that her words sounded very much the same as those Hayley had used the day before. "For now, he won't be coming back, that much he has made pretty clear, and I have the future to think of."

She manipulated a small cabinet to the top of the cellar steps.

"Now why don't you two go upstairs and play music or something, and let me get this straight. Then I'll do you pizzas."

"And that's another thing," said Livi. "My piano is in the den—I can't practise with you churning out gnomes and fairies all day long. But of course, I suppose my musical career can go on hold while you install some poxy lodger!"

Until that moment, Livi had had no intention whatever of making music her career, but if it would make her mother think again it was worth saying.

Judy held up her hands.

"It's all organised," she said. "A man is coming next Monday to put the piano in the sitting room—you can practise in there."

"It'll need tuning if you're going to move it," snapped Livi.

"I know, dear," smiled Judy sweetly through gritted teeth. "Len Griffiths is coming at 8:30 on Tuesday. Satisfied?"

Livi grunted.

"Hey, come on Livi," said Poppy eager to break the atmosphere which she could feel building by the second, "you've got to tell me all about this guy, remember?"

"What guy?" asked Judy attempting to take a maternal interest. "Fallen for someone new, have you, Livi?"

"It's no one you know," said Livi firmly. "You sort your life and let me get on with living mine."

And feeling marginally better for her riposte, she dragged Poppy upstairs to her room.

livi makes
a decision

"**S**o what else is new?" asked Poppy, lying stretched out on Livi's bed and flicking idly through a copy of *Lovelines*.

They had discussed in minute detail every exquisite feature of the amazing Ryan, and Poppy had solemnly sworn to do all in her power to track down his boat and then to invite Livi to walk casually up and down the towpath in her lime green mini-skirt. Livi had told her about Mr. Golding's total disinterest in her inability to organise the concert and Poppy had insisted that there was nothing to worry about.

"You just delegate," she said. "You decide what you want done and get someone else to do it. Easy!"

It occurred to Livi that Poppy would make

crossing the Sahara on a unicycle sound easy.

She had enlightened Poppy about her father's move to Leehampton and they had agreed that while the presence of Rosalie was to be deplored, Livi would simply have to persuade her mother to get her act together and use every ruse to lure Mike back to her.

"There's a book you can get which tells you how to use body language to arouse passion," said Poppy. "It's in BookEnds—you should get it and leave it somewhere obvious."

"Brilliant!" said Livi. "Anything's worth a try."

Poppy nodded.

"Of course," she added wisely, "it might not work. Maybe their destiny lies in other directions." Poppy was a profound believer in matters astrological.

The idea of her parents remaining apart forever was not one upon which Livi wished to dwell.

"I'm going to The Stomping Ground on Saturday," she said, in an attempt to change the subject.

Poppy looked surprised.

"I can't go," she said. "It's Mum's birthday and we're going for a meal at Gee Whizz to celebrate. Sorry," she added.

"That's OK," said Livi, surveying a leather skirt on the centre spread of *Yell!* and deciding it would make her look like a tree trunk. "I'm going with Hayley and Tamsin and that lot."

Poppy chucked her magazine onto the floor and sat up.

"You never used to hang around with them," she said accusingly.

"I know," said Livi. "That's because I spent all my time with you—but now that you're not there, it gets lonely. Do you miss me too?" she asked.

"Of course I do," said Poppy. "It's OK at school, though, because there's Victoria and Kim and this guy called Dex—"

"Called *what?*" interrupted Livi.

"Dex," said Poppy. "He's American and he is to die for."

"I thought you were still going out with Luke," said Livi accusingly. Poppy had finally fallen for Luke Cunningham, just around the time that Livi had stopped trying to push them together.

Poppy shrugged.

"I am," she said, "sort of. But that doesn't stop me being friendly with Dex as well. He thinks I'm really cool—he said so!"

"So when *do* you really miss me?" asked Livi persistently.

"Oh, when I'm shopping and feel like doing a makeover on someone; when I want to talk about the meaning of life and when there's no one to gossip with about all the people at Bellborough." She jumped off the bed. "Hey, why don't you show me what you're going to wear tomorrow night?"

She pulled open Livi's wardrobe door without asking and began rummaging among the hangers.

"Do you mind?" said Livi. "I tidied that yesterday."

"Sorry," Poppy looked abashed. "You never used to mind."

Livi grinned.

"I don't really—go on!" she encouraged. But as Poppy began to mutter, "No, not that," and "I don't think so somehow," at every other garment, she began to feel just a little bit miffed.

"I'm getting something new," said Livi. "Dad gave me £20."

"Brill!" said Poppy. "I know, why don't I come shopping with you? You know how timid you are when it comes to colour."

That's true, thought Livi.

"And in the right things, you can look well stunning," added Poppy. "If you haven't got enough cash, you can come back to my house and I'll lend you something," she said. "It would be like old times."

But suddenly, much as she loved Poppy, and scared as she was of choosing the wrong thing to wear, she knew it couldn't be like old times. Hayley was right; she was fourteen years old and she had to start being her own person. If she went on allowing Poppy to make all her decisions, she would never get anywhere. She wanted to be like Tamsin and Abby, full of confidence and never giving a toss for anyone else's opinion. She didn't want to be dependent on someone else to sort her out. She wasn't Poppy Field—she was Olivia Jacintha Hunter, shortly to become the adored girlfriend of Ryan . . . She stopped. She didn't even know his surname and here she was fantasising about how overnight she was going to turn into a self-confident, utterly desirable creature with whom Ryan would fall irretrievably in love. She was being stupid. Poppy was right—she was always going to need someone to point her in the right direction.

"Livi? Where shall we meet? For me to get you sorted?"

Had Poppy asked where they could meet to go shopping, Livi would have fallen in with her plans. But she didn't want to be sorted by Poppy, or by anyone else. If there was any sorting to do, she had to start doing it herself.

"Thanks a lot," she said, beaming at Poppy. "But I've already made plans for tomorrow morning. Maybe another week?"

It occurred to Livi that it was a very long time since she had seen Poppy so lost for words.

purchase points

By eleven o'clock on Saturday morning, being independent didn't seem so attractive to Livi. She had been in the Arndale Centre for two hours and tried on loads of gear but nothing seemed quite right. All she had managed to buy were two fetish bangles with little turquoise bears hanging from them and a stick of concealer. If she didn't find something soon, she'd have to go home to meet her dad—and have nothing to wear to The Stomping Ground. She began to wish she'd let Poppy take charge.

She was standing in Togs 'n' Clogs with a pair of bronze PVC hipsters in one hand and a lace shirt in the other wishing she was three inches taller and half a stone lighter when she caught sight of Tasha Reilly hovering in the doorway of the shop opposite, glancing up and down the centre anxiously.

Ramming the clothes back on the rail, she dashed across the mall towards her.

"Hi, Tasha!" she called, dodging a woman with a twin pushchair and two exceedingly irate toddlers. "I need your advice!"

Tasha jumped and looked alarmed.

"Oh, Livi, hi!" she said, glancing over her shoulder into the shop. "You going in?" She gestured behind her.

Livi shook her head. "I'm on a desperate mission and you have to help me," she said dramatically, not noticing the expression of relief on Tasha's face in her haste to enlist her help. "Come and tell me whether these trousers I've seen look all right on me."

Tasha looked uncertain.

"I can't, I'm waiting for Adam, actually and . . ."

"That's OK—it's only over here. You can watch out for him—please, it's desperate!"

She grabbed Tasha's arm and pulled her protesting into the boutique.

"Look," she said, grabbing the pair of PVC hipsters, "I was thinking maybe these . . . ?"

"No," said Tasha, shaking her head. "Your legs are the wrong shape."

"Oh thanks," muttered Livi.

"This?" She held up the lace shirt.

Tasha shook her head, her eyes scanning the rail.

"This!" declared Tasha, handing her a cord zip-up mini-dress the colour of ripening damsons.

"I can't wear that!" declared Livi. "I'd look . . ."

"Yes, you would," said Tasha, more decisively than Livi had ever heard her. "It'll look great. Try it on."

Livi retreated reluctantly to the changing room. Two minutes later, she emerged with a grin on her face.

"Tasha, it's brill—Tasha?" She glanced round the crowded shop. She couldn't see Tasha anywhere. Maybe she'd found something to try on herself.

She queued at the cash desk and paid for her

dress, but there was still no sign of Tasha. She must have left to find Adam.

Glancing at her watch, Livi realised that she only had ten minutes to get to the bus station. She pushed her way out of the shop and through the mall towards the exit. As she rounded the corner by The Toasted Teacake, she saw Tasha ahead of her. She was carrying a red shiny carrier bag and walking so fast that Livi had to break into a run to catch up with her.

"You were right!" she began, tapping Tasha on the shoulder. "That dress—it was amazing . . ."

She stopped. Tasha had spun round, and the expression on her face was one of sheer terror.

"Tasha? What's the matter?"

Tasha took a deep breath and shook her head dismissively.

"Nothing's the matter—why do you always keep asking me what's wrong?" she snapped. "You gave me a fright, that's all."

It crossed Livi's mind that having someone tap you on the shoulder in a packed shopping centre on a Saturday morning wasn't all that alarming, but she didn't say anything.

"Well, anyway, thanks—I would never tried on that colour in a million years!" she said. "It looks great."

"I knew it would," said Tasha, smiling briefly but quickening her pace.

"What have you bought?" asked Livi. "Let's see." She put her hand onto the bag and tried to peer inside.

"Look, just mind your own business, can't you?" shouted Tasha, snatching the bag away. "What's it to you what I've bought?"

"Sorry," said Livi, surprised at Tasha's reaction. Most of her mates were only too eager to show off their purchases. "I just thought you might have bought something for tonight."

"Tonight?" queried Tasha, frowning.

"The Stomping Ground," elaborated Livi, as they walked out of the centre into the Market Square. "You are going, aren't you?"

Tasha shrugged her shoulders.

"Haven't decided," she said. "I doubt it."

"Oh come on, it'll be cool," said Livi, who was rather dreading the whole thing herself and thought that having someone else in the same boat might make things easier. "Adam's going. Why don't you . . . ?"

"Look," shouted Tasha, with a shake in her voice, "just leave it, will you? If I want to go I will, and if I don't, I won't. OK? There's Adam—I must go."

And she ran across the cobbles to where Adam was leaning against a lamp post looking utterly delectable and rather bored.

"Suit yourself," muttered Livi under her breath and headed off to the bus station. It wasn't until she was on the bus that she realised that when Tasha had picked out the dress for Livi, she hadn't been carrying any shopping at all. Whatever it was that she had bought, she had done it very quickly.

livi tries it on

By half past twelve, Livi was perched on the windowsill in what had been, until her mother's latest madcap scheme, her father's den. She was practising an oboe concerto and watching out for his car, because the moment she spotted him, she intended to be out of the house and down the steps in a flash. There was no way she wanted him to see what her mother had done; it would probably break his heart, and besides, it would send out all the wrong messages. The room was now cluttered with bins of clay and pots of paint, and where her father's desk had been, there stood a huge trestle table covered in oilcloth. Even her father's favourite picture of Highland cattle standing by a stream had disappeared, and in its place was an extraordinary painting of arrows and splodges called

"Unstable Equilibrium," which Livi thought described her mother exactly.

Glancing round the untidy room, it occurred to Livi that instead of trying to make her father feel cherished and needed, it was as if her mother had tried to erase every trace of him. And Livi hated it.

She was seriously concerned that her mother was taking leave of her senses. She knew it happened to middle-aged women—only the week before Poppy had said that her mother had put the ironing in the freezer and a bumper pack of frozen chipolatas in the airing cupboard. It wasn't until her father complained that his shirts smelt revolting that the mistake was discovered.

But her mother's ridiculous idea of taking a lodger was a lot more serious than a packet of rancid sausages. She obviously wasn't thinking straight. Never mind that when they moved to Silverdale Road, Livi had wanted the back bedroom for her own, and had been told she couldn't have it because the light was perfect for painting fine detail onto fairy wings; never mind that her mother, who only last week had said that £39.99 for a fake fur jacket was out of the question, appeared not to be turning a hair at the idea of buying bedroom furniture for a total stranger. What really got to Livi was that she hadn't been consulted. Her mother had made an arbitrary decision without once asking Livi how she felt. Not, she thought miserably, fiddling with a curtain tie-back and wishing her dad would hurry up, that her feelings seemed to matter to anyone anymore.

That morning, while her mum had been hurtling in and out of the house, packing up her car with stuff to sell at the craft fair, Livi had tried a different ploy to get her mother to change her mind.

"I'm really worried about my school work," she had said, adopting what she hoped was a careworn expression.

"What on earth for?" asked her mother, wedging a grinning pixie between two sleeping cherubs. "You're doing fine."

"Yes, but with someone else in the house, and all the extra noise and everything . . ."

Her mother had roared with laughter, which

was not the reaction Livi had intended.

"You make it sound as if half of Leehampton Brass Band will be staying in the spare bedroom," she had joked, straightening up and grinning at Livi.

"Nice try, sweetheart, but for someone who can work out mathematical equations to a background of heavy metal, I hardly think one lodger is going to be much of a disturbance."

Livi had ignored the implication and tried again.

"Didn't you know that adolescents are meant to see their home as a haven from the pressures of growing up in a confused world?" she had said, quoting Mrs. Joll, who had very set views on the merits of a stable environment. "You're supposed to be giving me security and peace and room to develop and . . ."

"And piano lessons and money for discos and new clothes and the rest!" Her mother planted a kiss on the top of Livi's head. "Must dash, sweetheart—and don't worry; it'll be fun. You'll see."

Livi considered that her mother had a very strange idea of fun.

revelations
from rosalie

By quarter to one, Livi was beginning to wonder whether her father had forgotten her. There was no sign of his ancient car—not that she would have needed to look for it. You could hear it coming a mile off. It was on its last legs and rattled like an old tin can. But, thought Livi, once her father found a new job he would be able to get something with a bit more class.

Like that one, she thought, watching a sleek maroon Audi pulling up to the house. She was surprised to see the car stop and a tall, raven-haired woman climb out. She was wearing a cerise shirt, a violently patterned sarong skirt, and a pair of pink espadrilles. She looked, Livi thought critically, as if she had just stepped out of a cheap advert for Hawaii. As the woman glanced uncertainly up at the house, Livi realised with horror that it was the Wretched Rosalie.

Livi grabbed her bag and opened the front door, just as Rosalie was about to press the bell.

"Livi! How lovely to see you again!" Rosalie leaned forward in a cloud of Joy to kiss Livi's cheek, but Livi ducked out of the way and left her, lips puckered, pecking at thin air.

"Where's Dad?" demanded Livi unsmilingly.

Rosalie laughed. "He's fine—his old rust bucket finally gave up the ghost this morning, so he sent me to collect you. Come on—the table's booked for half past one and we'll pick up your dad on the way."

"You're coming too?" Livi knew it sounded rude but she had expected to have her father all to herself.

"You bet I am!" said Rosalie, pushing her black hair behind her ears, from which swung two huge earrings shaped like barracuda. "The only thing that's kept me going all morning scrubbing skirting boards in our new house was the thought of a decent meal!"

She opened the passenger door and stood back to let Livi climb in.

Our house. It sounded so—so married, thought Livi. And they weren't married. They shouldn't even be together. She hoped their crummy house would fall down round their ears and that Rosalie would be buried alive in the rubble.

As Rosalie clicked in her seat belt and started the engine, Livi glanced round the car. It smelt expensive, a mixture of new leather and polish.

"Nice, isn't it?" said Rosalie, pulling away from the kerb. "Picked it up this morning—it's one of the perks of the new job."

Livi looked up in surprise.

"Dad's got a new job already?" she gasped. "That's fantastic!"

Rosalie roared with laughter.

"Not Mike, silly—me!" she said. "Didn't he tell you?"

Livi bit her lip and shook her head. Who did this woman think she was, calling her silly?

"That's the main reason we decided to move back down here," Rosalie explained, as she swung the car smoothly into Wellington Road. "I got head hunted for Accounts Manager with the *Leehampton Echo*. I start next week. I'd been wanting to come back to the town for ages—my mum and my sister and her family live over in Kettleborough—but I suppose I thought, you know, with your mum and everything . . ." She hesitated.

"Oh, so you did think about my mother!" snapped Livi. "Like how you stole her husband and wrecked our lives and . . ."

"Hey, hang on a minute!" Rosalie glanced in the rearview mirror and pulled into the inside lane. "When I met your dad, and we fell for one another, it was me who asked for a transfer to Runcorn just because I didn't want to be the cause of any breakup!" she said. "Your dad came after me, not the other way round."

Livi swallowed. She didn't know that.

Rosalie laid a hand on her arm.

"I'm sorry—this must be foul for you," she said. "Anyway, when your dad got made redundant—" She paused. "He did tell you about the redundancy, didn't he?"

Livi nodded.

"Well, the job at the *Echo* was just too good to pass up," she said. "After all, someone's got to bring in the cash."

"Dad will land a job really easily," said Livi defensively. "He knows heaps of people."

Rosalie smiled.

"Let's hope so," she said easily.

Livi turned and stared out of the passenger window. There was an uncomfortable knot in her chest. Dad had said that they were moving down because he missed her so much. But it seemed that wasn't true. The only reason they had come was because of Rosalie's new job and the fact that she wanted to be nearer to her family. *Wanted them more than Dad wanted me*, thought Livi miserably. If she'd landed a job in Aberdeen, he would probably have gone dashing off there without a backward glance.

"Here we are," said Rosalie brightly. "That's us—the one with the red garage door."

Livi's eyes widened. Rosalie had turned into Billing Hill, which was what estate agents called an executive development, full of elegant houses with large gardens.

"It's big!" gasped Livi, gazing at the double-fronted red brick house in awe.

"It is a bit, isn't it?" said Rosalie apologetically. "I told Mike we didn't really need anything quite so lavish—we're only renting until, well, until things get sorted. But he insisted, so here we are!"

As Livi climbed out of the car, her father straightened up from under the bonnet of his blue Granada and waved.

"Welcome to Copperbeech," he said with a mock flourish. "Isn't it just great!

"Take a look inside, Livi, while I wash my hands. Then we'll pop over to The Snooty Fox."

The house was beautiful. Not only was there a huge sitting room with a marble fireplace, and a dining room opening onto the garden, but there was a wood-panelled study and a kitchen with a pine table and wooden airers hanging from the ceiling.

A broad, dog-leg staircase led upstairs.

"And we thought you could sleep in here when you stay over," said Rosalie, throwing open a door to reveal a large room decorated in peach and apple green. "Your dad and I really do want you to feel that this is your second home—you could stay over when your mum has to go away and . . ."

How Mum would like to be able to afford a house like this, thought Livi. And a picture of her mother earlier that day, with lines of tiredness round her eyes, loaded down with boxes of gnomes and wizards, staggering down the steps to the car, flashed before her eyes.

She looked at Rosalie.

"Thank you," she said icily, "but I have a perfectly nice home of my own. With my mother."

It gave her enormous satisfaction to see Rosalie flush a livid shade of lobster and even more to see how horribly it clashed with her shirt.

"Now, you two sit there and get to know one another, and I'll get us some drinks." Mike Hunter ushered Rosalie and Livi to a corner table in The Snooty Fox. "What will you have, Livi?"

"Coke, I bet," said Rosalie.

Livi, who had been on the point of asking for just that, changed her mind.

"Seven Up, please," she said.

"And your usual, my luvvyluv," he said to Rosalie, and Livi cringed at the infantile term of endearment.

"Well," said Rosalie brightly, in an attempt to break the wall of silence that followed Mike's departure to the bar. "How's school?"

She clapped her hand to her mouth. "Oh no, I don't believe I just said that! What a naff question! When I was your age I vowed I would never ever ask anyone how they were getting on at school and now I've done just that."

Livi said nothing but stared resolutely at the menu.

I hate this woman, she thought miserably.

"You must hate me," remarked Rosalie, and Livi, stunned that she was echoing her own thoughts, looked up startled.

Rosalie grinned.

"I don't blame you really," she said in a matter-of-fact manner. "I mean, you know hardly anything about me and here I am with your dad, making asinine remarks and trying to win you over when you would probably prefer to see me being demolished by a ten-ton truck." She unfolded her napkin. "Or slowly suffocating in a fast-moving quicksand."

Despite herself, Livi felt the corners of her mouth twitch. At least Rosalie wasn't trying to pretend that they were the best of mates.

"So you like our new house?" asked Mike, dumping three drinks on the table.

"It's not yours, it's just rented," remarked Livi acerbically. Rosalie and Mike exchanged glances.

"Well, yes," agreed her father, "but it's a bit special, isn't it? Shows the world Mike Hunter is on the up again."

Rosalie took a sip of wine.

"Shows the world that Rosalie Cutler is working bloody hard," she said.

Oh good, thought Livi. Discord. And felt more hopeful than she had all day.

table talk

"So what have you been doing with yourself?" Livi's father asked her, as they tucked into their main courses. "Any more music exams coming up?"

Livi shook her head.

"Worse than that," she said. "Old Golding's only gone and put me in charge of organising some stupid concert for this two hundredth anniversary Gala Weekend. I told him I couldn't do it, but he wouldn't listen."

"Oh, of course you can do it!" said her father, taking a gulp of red wine. "No problems."

Rosalie laid down her knife and fork and looked at Livi.

"That must be quite a worry for you," she said thoughtfully. "I mean, I know you are great at music and everything, but coming up with ideas and licking other people into shape—well, that's something else altogether, isn't it?"

CHAPTER FOURTEEN

Livi nodded, surprised that someone like Rosalie would pick up on the problem so easily.

"I don't mind finding the music, and I love playing. I'd even write some stuff, if it comes to that," she admitted. "It's just that I am totally useless at organisation."

"Nonsense, you'll be just great!" interjected her father, vigorously slicing a sirloin steak. "It's an honour."

"Honour or not, Dad, I really am getting in a state about it," she said. "It's only a few weeks away, and I don't even know where to begin."

"Lists," said Rosalie, spiking a mushroom.

"Pardon?" asked Livi.

"Lists," repeated Rosalie. "I swear by them. I'm hopelessly disorganised until I write something down. Then, as long as I have a 'must be done by' date and 'person who's going to do it' slot, I'm fine!"

Livi sighed.

"That sounds like a good idea," she admitted somewhat grudgingly. "Except I can't even think up the things that have to go on the lists in the first place! It's all got to be about the founding of the school and the orphans that were the first pupils and how life was in those days. And I'm not even any good at history!" she added.

"Nonsense!" exclaimed her father. "You're just saying that—I know you!"

You don't know me at all really, thought Livi and immediately felt ashamed that such a thought should have crossed her mind.

"You got any ideas, Dad?" she asked, trying to appease her conscience.

"One very good one," he said.

"Yes?" breathed Livi eagerly. Any idea would be a start.

"Double Death by Chocolate, followed by a large cappuccino." He turned to Rosalie. "What do you say, my luvvyluv?"

As they strolled back to the car, Rosalie, who had not been very talkative towards the end of the meal, turned to Livi.

"Look," she said briskly, "I don't want to interfere and heaven knows, you probably want to see as little of me as you possibly can, but if you get in a jam with this concert thing, or need someone to brainstorm with, you know where I am."

Livi opened her mouth to protest but Rosalie kept on talking.

"You probably won't need any help at all. But I read like a thing possessed and have hundreds of books and cuttings that might just be useful to you when it comes to thinking up the initial ideas." She paused, brow puckered. "Two hundred years? So that means the school was founded in—what? 1797?"

Livi nodded.

"Brilliant!" exclaimed Rosalie.

"It is?" Livi looked exceedingly doubtful.

"Oh yes," cried Rosalie enthusiastically. "You can have a bit about Jenner discovering about inoculation against smallpox, and then there's old Bonaparte leaping about all over Europe, and then of course just a few years on, there was the big Health Act that meant paupers didn't have to work for more than twelve hours at a stretch in the factories . . ."

"Twelve hours!" Livi gasped.

"Awful when you think how people moan

today if they don't get three coffee breaks and ninety minutes for lunch!" laughed Rosalie.

"How come you know so much?" asked Livi who was becoming so interested that she forgot to be stand-offish.

Rosalie shrugged.

"I don't know that much really," she said. "I just find history intensely fascinating and read everything I can lay my little mitts on." She glanced across the car park. "Come on, Mike's got his impatient face on!"

Livi's dad was standing by the car door tapping his foot up and down on the gravel.

"Come on you two," he said. "It's great to see that you are getting on so well, but I have to drop Livi back. She's got a hot date, haven't you, Livi?"

Livi glared at him.

"It's not a date, Dad, just a night out with some mates," she mumbled.

"Oh come on, now," he chuckled, reversing the car out onto the road, "you don't expect me to believe that one, do you?"

Rosalie turned to face Livi who was in the back seat.

"In my day, the gang evenings were always the best," she said. "None of that awful 'Oh my God has he seen my zit?' stuff."

This time Livi laughed out loud.

It wasn't until Livi was back home, standing in front of her mirror and wondering whether she should telephone Poppy to ask what colour shoes would go with her damson dress, that the thought struck her. She had always thought of Rosalie as the total dimbo, but today it had actually been her own father who had made the stupidest remarks.

leonora
descends

Livi was exhausted. Very probably she wouldn't have the energy to stand, let alone dance, at The Stomping Ground. Just after she had got home, Hayley had phoned in something of a tizz.

"Hi, Livi. Look, my stepdad can't drive us to the SG after all—something about some meeting. Can your mum do it?"

Livi hesitated.

"She's at the craft fair right now, and she won't be back before six," she began. Knowing what her mother was usually like after a day on her feet, Livi was not altogether sure that she would jump at the idea.

"That's OK, she could pick me up at seven—Tim's meeting me at the SG after rugby," she added.

"She's usually shattered and not in the best of moods," warned Livi.

"Oh, she won't mind, will she? Do the stressed-out daughter bit, remember? My stepdad says he'll bring us all home."

"Well, I suppose I could ask her."

"Terrific! Thanks a bunch, Livi. See you at my house at seven. Cheers!"

Since then Livi had been tearing round the house like a thing possessed. She had put the kettle on ready to offer her mother a calming cup of camomile, vacuumed the carpets, and even tidied her bedroom. Well, not tidied exactly. She had kicked all the shoes and books and CDs that were on the floor under her bed, and hurled everything else into the bottom drawer of her chest and rammed it shut.

In a final gesture that even she had to admit was nothing short of brilliant, she had put up the ironing board in the kitchen, switched on the iron and spread one of her mother's cotton shirts across the board. She wasn't so desperate that she intended to begin ironing until she had an audience.

She was just putting the finishing touches to her make-up and deciding that somehow her mother would have to be persuaded to pay for her to go to Fringe Affairs for proper highlights when she heard her mother's car pull up outside.

She flew down the stairs, into the kitchen, grabbed the iron, slammed it on the shirt and tried to look like a caring, thoroughly domesticated daughter.

"Well, here we are," she heard her mother's voice chirrup into the hallway. She was even talking to herself now. It was sad.

Livi waited in anticipation of her mother's delight at seeing her tackle the ironing—delight which would, of course, preclude all denial about an eight-mile round trip to The Stomping Ground—but Judy didn't appear. Instead another voice joined hers in the hallway.

"Hey, Judy, this is so incredible—will you just look at those fairies?" The voice was very obviously American. "And that pixie—he is just *dah-ling!*"

There were a few clatters and bangs and then Livi heard her mother's voice.

"Come upstairs and see the room—and then we'll go through to the kitchen."

Heavy steps could be heard disappearing upstairs.

The lodger. That voice must belong to a prospective lodger. Livi sank down onto a chair. And to think she had spent the last half hour making the house look a million dollars. If she'd known, she could have scruffed it up and put this person off.

From upstairs came peals of laughter. Perhaps, thought Livi hopefully, it was a hoot of derision at the total unsuitability of the room.

Livi crept to the bottom of the stairs.

"It's just the cutest room and so right for what I need," said the voice. "You just found yourself a lodger."

Oh sugar, thought Livi. And sniffed. The ironing!

"I'll go down and make some tea and you come when you're ready," she heard her mother say, and hurtled into the kitchen and grabbed the iron. It wasn't a very large burn. She turned the shirt over just as her mum pushed open the door.

"Oh, there you are, sweetheart," beamed Judy, giving her a hug. "Did you have a nice time with your dad?"

"It was OK," said Livi non-committally, not wanting to get her mother upset.

Judy eyed the ironing board.

"Getting your gear ready for tonight?" She wrinkled her nose and peered closer at the shirt. "Isn't that mine?"

Livi nodded miserably.

"I was trying to help—I did the vacuuming and tidied my room and the kettle's on and then I thought I'd do your ironing, only I heard voices and came . . ." She stopped and held up the damaged shirt, steeling herself for the explosion.

Judy grinned amiably.

"Don't worry—it was a nice thought and I only wear that old thing for work anyway," she said. She pulled open a drawer, took out an incense stick and stuck it into a ceramic Buddha who stood grinning on the windowsill.

"I think," she whispered conspiratorially, striking a match and lighting the incense, "that we've got ourselves a lodger."

There's no need to sound so chuffed about it, thought Livi, coughing as a waft of patchouli hit her nostrils. This could be the end of civilised life as we know it.

"Mum, are you sure this is a good idea?" she ventured politely, remembering the need to keep on the right side of her mother for another hour at least.

"Positive," said Judy emphatically. "This morning my stars said that my finances would receive a boost and that I would meet a woman who would transform my future. Well, I sold £156 worth of stuff, and took orders for £400 more, and then, when I stopped for lunch . . ."

"She met me!" Livi turned. Standing in the doorway, dressed in a capacious russet-coloured wool trouser suit and with what appeared to be half the nation's gold reserves round her neck, was a large, very beautiful woman with a plump face and a mass of unruly auburn hair.

"Hi!" she said, beaming at Livi and offering a hand groaning under the weight of rings the size of small conkers. "I'm Leonora—Leonora Tadcaster. And you must be Olivia!" She clasped her hand and shook it vigorously, her assorted items of jewellery rattling enthusiastically.

"Well now," she sighed, casting an eye around the kitchen, "is this just the neatest thing?"

Livi tried not to laugh. She was so—everywhere.

Judy stepped forward.

"Leonora's going to be renting the back bedroom," she said. "Just for a few weeks while she works on a book."

"You're an author?" asked Livi, thinking that if they had to have a lodger it might do her street cred a bit of good to have someone famous.

"Sure am," said Leonora pushing up the sleeves of her jacket to reveal a cluster of gold bracelets. "I write children's books—you know the *Ghosts of Glossops Glen* series?"

Livi made a non-committal noise in her throat which she hoped might pass for a yes.

"Anyway, right now I'm over here in good old England to start a whole new series—*The Canal Clan*—with my sister, Cordelia French. Such fun—she's doing the illustrations, I do the words."

121 ✳

She sank down in a chair and stretched her legs out in front of her.

"That's how I found out about the room—I was helping Cordy sell some paintings at the craft fair and moaning on and on about how impossible it is to write in a hotel bedroom, and there like an angel sent from high was your darling mom, offering the solution to all my dilemmas!"

She clapped her hands together like a delighted child.

"And you're sure you wouldn't be more comfortable staying with your sister?" Judy asked anxiously.

Leonora threw back her head and roared with laughter.

"No way!" she chuckled. "Cordelia may be a wonderful artist but she's totally impossible to live with! Anyway, she prefers to be left in peace to paint. No, I shall just scribble away here and then trot off and liaise with Cordy over a bottle of something red when necessary. She's best taken in small doses and with alcohol!" She slapped her hand on the table and laughed again.

The kitchen clock chimed half past six.

"A glass of wine to celebrate, Leonora?" Judy opened the fridge and took out a bottle of Australian Chardonnay.

Hang on, thought Livi. You've got the chauffeuring bit to do yet.

"Mum, I know you're tired and everything, but you see, Hayley's stepdad can't take us to The Stomping Ground and I wondered . . ." she tailed off, waiting for the vociferous denial.

"The Stomping what?" Leonora interjected.

"The Stomping Ground," said Livi curtly, annoyed at being interrupted when she was in the middle of the well-mannered daughter bit. "It's a disco."

"I must use it," said Leonora and dived into her capacious scarlet handbag, fished out a spiral notebook, and began scribbling. "Wonderful name—might make a title. Sorry, do carry on!"

Livi reset her features in a pleading expression.

"So you see . . ." she began.

Judy turned to her, corkscrew in hand.

"What you're saying is that you want a lift?" she said.

Livi nodded, waiting for the "I've been on my feet all day and now you expect to drive across town" bit.

"Fine. What time do we need to leave?"

Livi stared at her.

"You mean—you will?"

Judy looked surprised.

"Of course," she said, as if disagreeing with her daughter had never been part of her agenda. "How many am I taking?"

Mum was obviously on something. She was never, ever this amenable.

"Just me and Hayley," she said.

"Fine," said Judy. "I have to drop Leonora off at the Riverside Hotel so that she can collect her things, anyway."

She turned to Leonora. "You don't mind, do you? We'll have the wine when you get back! Ready in five minutes, Livi?"

If I had known she was going to be in this good a mood, thought Livi, I could have spared myself all that vacuuming.

livi takes the plunge

"**D**o I look all right?" Livi tugged at her mini-dress which suddenly seemed to have shortened itself by three inches at the same time as her thighs had doubled in size. "I'm not sure about this chain—and my hair? Should I put it . . ."

Hayley grabbed her wrist and dragged her through the door of The Stomping Ground.

"You look great," she shouted above the noise of the latest Blur track. "Stop worrying—just chill and have a ball!"

An hour later, Livi had come to the conclusion that chilling was not her strong point. Hayley was spending all her time with Tim, and Tamsin was on what she called a guy chase, chatting up everyone she liked the look of and dashing back to the table every so often to encourage Livi to do the same.

"I can't," protested Livi, "I'm not like you—I can't just go up to some guy I don't know and start chatting."

"Why not?" demanded Tamsin, smoothing a hand across her hair. "They don't bite—well, not to start with anyway," she said with a suggestive giggle and slid off to corner an ebony-haired guy with a ponytail.

Abigail, who was wearing a minuscule black lace dress and a large quantity of mocha lipstick, had arrived late with Adam and made a great display of entering with her arms wrapped around him. They had spent the past half hour dancing and Adam in particular was in exceedingly high spirits, leaping about, waving his arms in the air and singing along with all the tracks. Abby repeatedly cast frequent glances over her shoulder to ensure that they had an audience. Of Tasha there was no sign.

"How you doing?" Hayley flopped down in a chair next to Livi. "Tim's talking rugby to some guys from the club." She sounded miffed that he could possibly find anything more fascinating than her company.

"Adam's on a high, isn't he?" she remarked, watching him punching the air in time to the beat.

Livi said nothing. He had never appeared to enjoy himself that much when he was with her.

Hayley grabbed Livi's arm. "I'm parched— let's get some more drinks."

It was as they stood up to go to the bar that Livi saw him. On the far side of the room, talking to a slim, curly-haired guy, was Ryan. She was sure it was. Her heart began to beat wildly and she stopped dead in her tracks.

"It's him," she muttered, nudging Hayley in the ribs.

"What's who?" asked Hayley, whose grasp of grammar always failed her in moments of high drama.

"Ryan—the guy I told you about, the one I met outside my house," Livi hissed. "There, in the turquoise shirt."

"Nice!" breathed Hayley. "Very, very nice. Well, what are you waiting for?"

"What?" said Livi.

"Go and talk to him," urged Hayley.

Livi was about to protest that she couldn't possibly do anything of the sort, when Abigail came sidling up, hanging on to Adam's arm and exuding a cloud of Anais Anais over the table.

"Livi, hi!" she simpered. "All alone as usual?"

"She needn't be," said Tamsin, appearing at her elbow. "I've tried to give her lessons in pulling but she's too chicken!"

"Poor Livi," said Adam in mock soothing tones, quite unlike his normal friendly nature.

That's it, thought Livi. I've had it with you lot.

"Sorry?" she said, pretending not to have heard the catty remarks. "I'll see you guys later—Ryan's here."

Her horror at her own audacity was tempered somewhat by the satisfaction of seeing the looks of sheer astonishment that flickered across the faces of her friends. Even Adam's eyes widened slightly as he scanned the room to see just who it was that Livi was referring to.

Somehow she propelled her legs across the

room, her heart thumping in her chest and prayed that she wouldn't make a total and complete idiot of herself.

Ryan was deep in conversation with his mate.

"Hi!" she said, so softly that he didn't hear her. The guy next to him gestured in her direction and Ryan turned round.

"Did you find the boat all right?" asked Livi, wishing she could think of a wittier way to start a conversation and wondering why her tongue felt as if it were stuck to the roof of her mouth.

"The boat?" Ryan frowned. "Oh—you're the girl from—Olivia, isn't it?"

Livi nodded.

Ryan grinned and Livi felt quite faint with desire.

"Yes, yes I did, thanks," he said. "Not before time, either. My mum had managed to get it stuck broadside on by the lock. She was not the most popular person."

He turned to his mate.

"Jon, this is Olivia—sorry, I don't know your surname."

"Hunter, Olivia Hunter."

Ryan stared at her.

"Hunter?" he repeated slowly. "Did you say Hunter?"

Livi nodded.

"Olivia Hunter," he repeated.

Livi wondered how long this name check was going on for.

"My friends call me Livi," she added.

"Well, Livi Hunter," said Ryan, looking at her with a great deal of interest, "why don't we dance?"

dream dish

Livi had felt as if she had died and gone to heaven. They had been dancing for only a few minutes, when the beat changed and a slow, smoochy number started up. Ryan put his arms around Livi and she saw out of the corner of her eye that the gang were watching her with a mixture of amazement and ill-concealed envy.

"This place isn't bad, is it?" he said, gesturing round the dimly lit disco. "Do you hang out here regularly?"

Livi shook her head.

"Not really," she admitted. "I came tonight because my friend Hayley persuaded me."

"I'm glad she did," said Ryan and Livi's heart did another unrestrained leap. "Must have been fate—I only found out about it this afternoon from Jon."

"Jon?"

"The guy I was chatting to," explained

Ryan, jerking his head in the direction of the bar. "Jon was down by the canal sketching for some 'A' level project and helped me get the boat tied up after Mum had done her Captain Pugwash bit."

Livi giggled. Tamsin, who was dancing with the ponytailed guy, shot her an enquiring glance. She smiled enigmatically and turned away.

"We got to talking and he suggested I come along. So here I am."

"It must be neat living on a boat," commented Livi, remembering the advice about taking an interest.

"It's all right for the summer," he said, "but I couldn't stand it for longer. Not enough space. We've got a bungalow in Kettleborough," he added, "but since my dad died, my mum likes to rent out the house in the summer and take to the water, as she calls it. She's an artist and they get these funny ideas," he added wryly.

"Don't I know it!" exclaimed Livi. "My mother does ceramics and she is totally mad! I'm sorry about your dad," she added gently.

Ryan took a deep breath.

"Thanks," he said, his face clouding briefly. "What about you? Is your dad still around?"

Well, he's alive, if that's what you mean, thought Livi.

"Yes," she said, not wanting to embark on a lengthy explanation of the ludicrous way in which her parents chose to conduct their lives.

Ryan looked interested.

"And what does he do?" he asked.

Livi hesitated.

"He's in marketing," she said. She thought that sounded better than "out of work salesman."

"Really?" Ryan appeared fascinated by this boring fact. "Who does he work for?"

Livi was just thinking that it was somewhat odd for a guy she had only just met to take such an acute interest, but was prevented from having to discuss her father when the music faded and the lights went up.

"Look," said Ryan, taking her hand, "why don't I get us some drinks and you can introduce me to your mates. If you don't mind, that is," he added.

Mind? thought Livi. It would give me the utmost pleasure.

"He is divine!" murmured Hayley, when Livi, flushed from both her exertions and the triumph of having done the unthinkable, returned to the corner table.

"Who was *that*?" asked Tamsin who had discarded the ponytail guy and was now eyeing Ryan with an experienced eye. "He is dreamy!"

"This is Ryan," said Livi, suddenly shy as Ryan came up to the table and handed her a drink. He would probably take one look at Tamsin and Hayley and forget she existed.

"Hi!" said Ryan, with the confidence of one used to having three pairs of female eyes glued on his face. "Are you all at school with Livi?"

Livi could have hugged him for the way he made it sound as if he had known her for ages.

In the conversation that followed, Livi discovered that he was sixteen, was doing his GCSEs at Kettleborough Grange School and played in a band called Plastic Pumpkin. Of course, she made it seem as if she knew all this already and noticed how Tamsin and Hayley hung on his every word.

She was just wishing she could have him to herself again when Abigail and Adam reappeared.

"Well, hi there!" cooed Abby, leaning towards Ryan and giving him her most winning smile. "I'm Abigail."

"Hi," said Ryan disinterestedly. He turned to Livi.

"Let's dance," he said.

It was, thought Livi, her greatest moment yet. She would remember the look on Abigail's face until the day she died.

livi falls
in love

By ten o'clock, Livi was wildly, passionately and irretrievably in love. She realised that every other boy she had ever fancied had merely been a childish infatuation; this was the Real Thing.

Ryan was so cool, so perfect; how she could ever have thought herself in love with the immature boys in her year she couldn't imagine. They talked about everything under the sun; he seemed keen to know all about her and asked whether she had brothers and sisters, and how long she had lived in Leehampton and what her favourite subjects were. In fact, Livi had never met a guy who seemed so interested in the mundane things of life.

"What's this band you play in?" Livi asked.

"Oh, it's just a bunch of us from school," he

said. "We started it to raise money on Red Nose Day and it just kind of took off from there. Do you like music?"

Livi nodded.

"I *love* music," she enthused. "I play anything, but I'm better at classical—the piano and oboe hardly lend themselves to heavy metal!"

Ryan grinned.

"My dad used to be in a band," added Livi. "I can only hope he was less embarrassing then than he is when he does his Elvis impressions at our Christmas parties . . ." She trailed off, thinking suddenly that this year Dad wouldn't be there to do Elvis or anything else.

"Your dad's musical? Really?" This piece of information appeared to cause Ryan an inordinate amount of delight. "What does he play?"

"Guitar," said Livi.

"Me too!" exclaimed Ryan. "That's amazing—I mean, it's an amazing coincidence."

They danced in silence for a minute and then Ryan looked down at her.

"Meeting you has been so cool," he said.

Perhaps it meant—please let it mean—that

he felt as she did and wanted to get to know her better.

When the lights went up and the DJ had announced that he was taking a short break, Ryan and Livi pushed their way back to the corner table to cool off. When Ryan took her hand and held on to it firmly, Livi felt a great shiver of delight, partly because of his touch and partly because she could see that her friends were totally gobsmacked at seeing Livi, whom they had always considered totally inept when it came to flirting, being chatted up by the most gorgeous guy in the building.

They had all just entered a fairly heated debate about the merits of Oasis over Crash Course Kids when there was a commotion at the door.

"Please, I have to get in—I have to find my brother!" Livi and Hayley both turned at the sound of the familiar voice. "Please, it's an emergency!"

It was Tasha, wearing loose baggy cotton trousers and a bright green shirt and looking frantically around the room, while the guy on the door tried to bar her from going in without a ticket.

"What's up with her?" said Tamsin. "And what *has* she got on?"

Livi was less concerned with Tasha's choice of outfit than with her very obvious distress.

"She's in my class," she said to Ryan, by way of explanation. "I'm going to find out what's going on."

"I'll come with you," said Ryan, pushing back his chair and standing up.

When they got to the door, Tasha was in tears.

"They won't let me in and I have to get Adam," she said. "Something awful has happened."

"I'll get him," offered Livi and darted back to the others. "Where's Adam?"

"He and Abby went outside about twenty minutes ago," said Tamsin. "They said they wanted fresh air, but I personally think . . ."

"Who cares what you think?" snapped Livi. "This is a crisis."

Tamsin opened and shut her mouth like a

perplexed goldfish. She'd never seen Livi disagree with anyone.

Ryan, Livi, and Tasha scanned the street outside but couldn't spot Adam or Abigail. Just as Tasha was dissolving into tears for the second time, Livi heard voices coming from a doorway across the road. Adam and Abby were sitting on a step drinking lemonade and giggling uncontrollably.

"There he is!" said Livi triumphantly. "Adam, come here—Tasha wants you!"

Adam stopped, bottle poised in the air and stared across the road. He didn't make any attempt to move.

"Weedy sister wants you!" chirped Abby and burst out laughing again.

"What's going on?" Hayley and Tamsin, curiosity having overcome them, joined them on the pavement.

"I think," said Ryan, turning to face them with a serious expression on his face, "that your friends have had rather too much to drink."

drama in
a doorway

Tasha darted across the road.

"Adam!" she cried tearfully, "You have to come home! It's Mum; she's been rushed to hospital."

Adam stared uncomprehendingly at her. Abby blinked and brushed a hand across her eyes.

"What *have* you got on?" sneered Abigail, and Livi realised that Tasha was dressed in *salwar kameez*.

Tasha ignored her and shook her brother's shoulder firmly.

"Adam? What's the matter with you? Didn't you hear what I said? Mum's ill!" she shouted.

Adam clambered a little unsteadily to his feet. The bottle rolled along the pavement and came to rest against Livi's left foot. She bent down to pick it up.

CHAPTER NINETEEN

"It's KickStart," she gasped disbelievingly. "Alcoholic fruit juice." She stared at her ex-boyfriend.

"Adam," she said in disgust, "you are a total idiot."

Adam peered at her as if having difficulty focusing on her face.

"Oh loosen up," he said. "What's the big deal?"

Ryan took the empty bottle out of Livi's hand, and hurled it with what appeared to be unnecessary force into a nearby waste bin.

"What do you . . ." Adam began, but Tasha interrupted.

"You have to get it together," she persisted, making no attempt to hide her tears. "Come on—Dadu and Dida are waiting in the car . . ." She gestured down the hill to where a dark green Jaguar was parked under a lamp post.

"*Don't* call them that!" Adam suddenly exploded into life. "I've told you—it's Gran and Grandad." He looked wildly round his group of friends. "She still calls them baby names," he began apologetically. "My grandmother . . ."

"Is waiting to take you to see your mother."

They all turned. An elegant dark-skinned woman with greying hair pulled tightly back into a bun on the nape of her neck had appeared at Livi's shoulder and stood looking coolly down at Adam and Abigail. She wore a jade green and gold sari and a cluster of gold bracelets jangled on her slender wrist.

Abigail scrambled to her feet, her mouth agape.

"You're Adam's grandmother?" she asked incredulously.

The woman inclined her head slightly.

"I am," she said. "And now, Adam, please—the car. Your mother has had a collapse. It is doubtless due to all the worry over . . ."

"I'm coming!" Adam interrupted hastily. He turned to Abigail.

"I'll phone you," he said.

Abby didn't reply. She just kept staring at Adam and Tasha's grandmother.

"Poor them," breathed Livi as the trio climbed into the car and drove away.

"I hope it's not serious," said Hayley. "A collapse sounds bad."

"Are you OK, Abby?" asked Tamsin, as Abby remained motionless, staring into space.

Abigail looked at them all in horror.

"I don't believe it," she said, running her fingers through her hair.

"Don't worry, I'm sure his mum will be . . ." began Livi, who despite not having a great deal of affection for Abby, could sympathise with how anxious she must be feeling.

"Never mind his mum!" snapped Abigail. "If that really was Adam's grandmother, you know what it means?"

The gang looked at her open-mouthed.

"I've been going out with an Indian!" She spat the words out with distaste. "My dad will kill me!"

Livi was the first to regain the power of speech.

"That's an awful thing to say!" she exclaimed. "What does it matter what nationality he is?"

Tamsin frowned. "Reilly doesn't sound much like an Indian surname to me," she muttered.

Hayley sighed. "Tam, you are mega dense at times," she said in her forthright manner. "His *father* is obviously English—or Irish, with a name like that—and his mum is Indian."

"A half caste!" Abigail wailed, as if it had just been discovered that Adam's family were cannibals.

"Abby!" The others expostulated in disbelief.

Ryan threw a look of distaste at Abigail and laid a hand on Livi's shoulder.

"Come on," he said, "It's almost eleven o'clock—and I want another dance before the end."

Livi momentarily forgot her anger and revelled in the fact that for once she would be on the floor at the end of a disco and not sitting staring at her reflection in a glass of Seven Up.

"That guy's a fool!" muttered Ryan as they pushed their way back onto the floor. "He's only a kid—he could do himself real damage with that stuff."

Livi had never thought of Adam as a kid before—but being with Ryan made everyone else seem positively childish.

"Seeing people out of control through alcohol just makes me so angry, I want to shake them till it hurts," said Ryan, clenching his fingers.

145 ✳

"I suppose it's not our problem," said Livi, wondering why Ryan was getting so heated over a guy he didn't even know.

"It *was* my problem," he said. "And my mother's, too. My dad was killed by a drunk driver," he added quietly.

"I'm so sorry," said Livi.

They danced in silence for a moment.

"What makes me mad is the way Abigail—that's the girl he's with—goes on," she shouted above the noise of the music. "How can people be like that? What does it matter who his mother is—or who his father is for that matter?"

"Sometimes it matters," he said softly under his breath, as if he was talking to himself.

"Pardon?"

"Nothing." Ryan shook his head. "Anyway, you can't just blame your friend; her parents must be pretty prejudiced for her to think like that."

"I suppose," agreed Livi.

Ryan smiled at her and pulled her closer. All thoughts of Abigail's prejudices and Tasha's mother fled from Livi's mind.

As the last track drew to a close, she started praying as hard as she knew how.

Please let him ask me out, she pleaded silently. Please. If you make this happen, God, I will never ask you for anything else ever again. Ever in my whole life. I promise.

Ryan coughed, swallowed and looked straight into her eyes.

"I really would like to see you again," he said. "If that would be all right."

"Oh yes," breathed Livi. "That would be fine. Absolutely fine."

Ryan leaned forward and kissed her lightly on the cheek.

"Great," he said. "After all, we do seem to have a lot in common."

As it turned out they had rather more in common than either of them knew.

mother
behaving
badly

"Bye, thanks for the lift!" Livi waved to Hayley's stepdad and sprang up the steps to her front door.

I'm in love, I'm in love, she chanted to herself. Suddenly she felt as if she could cope with anything the world hurled at her. She might even manage to write the odd song for the school concert. Although somehow she didn't think *Love Song to Ryan* would be very relevant to a musical history of Bellborough Court.

Ryan was going to phone her. Ryan wanted to see her again. She let herself in the front door and glimpsed her reflection in the mirror.

I even look almost pretty, she thought in amazement.

CHAPTER TWENTY

"Mum! I'm home!" she called. From the sitting room came the sound of giggling.

"Oh, Judy, you don't need a man!" she heard Leonora declare. "More trouble than they are worth. Believe me, you're better off without him!"

This, thought Livi, would not do at all. Her mother didn't need any encouragement to forget her father. She had known that having a lodger could only lead to trouble.

"You could be right!" laughed her mum, sounding exceedingly cheerful for someone suffering from a broken heart.

Livi pushed open the sitting room door and gawped in amazement.

Her mother and Leonora were sprawled in armchairs, her mother in her blue velour dressing gown, and Leonora in a voluminous caftan in a most alarming shade of apricot. They were both holding glasses of red wine and looking somewhat flushed. A row of chunky yellow candles was burning on the mantelpiece, and a large Victorian mirror that Livi recognised as having once been on her mother's bedroom wall was now hanging in the corner.

"Sweetheart! You're home!" Her mother beamed at her. "Had a good evening?"

"Yes thanks," Livi replied, eyeing them critically. "What's with the candles?"

"Feng shui," said her mother.

"Fen what?"

Leonora waved a jewel-bedecked hand in the air.

"Feng shui," she said. "Acupuncture for houses."

"We've been harnessing energy," said Judy. "Leonora knows all about it—she brought the candles."

"Yellow," elaborated Leonora. "For joy and conviviality."

"It seems to me," said Livi loftily, "that you don't need much help on the conviviality front. And what's with the bedroom mirror being down here?"

"Disaster area," declared Leonora. "Your mother could see herself in it as she lay in bed." She took another sip of wine. "Very energy draining, absolute feng shui no-no."

Oh cripes, thought Livi, what sort of a nut-case have we got here?

Her mother picked up the wine bottle and shared the remaining dregs between herself and Leonora.

"You've had quite enough of that," said Livi sternly. "Do you realise what that stuff does to you?" An uncomfortable image of Adam and Abigail floated before her eyes.

"Oh darling, don't be so stuffy," laughed her mother. "We've only had a drop and it's not as if we're driving or anything. Now, tell us all about your evening. Meet anyone nice?"

"Actually, I did," said Livi.

"Oh super fun," enthused Leonora. She patted the arm of her chair. "Sit here and tell all."

Judy nodded.

"Come on, sweetheart—was he a dish?"

Livi surveyed her inebriated parent with disdain.

"I will tell you about it when you are in a more sensible frame of mind. I'm going to bed. Good night."

"Night night sweetheart," cooed her mother.

"Sweet dreams," echoed Leonora.

Rather impressed by her new-found sophistication, Livi closed the door and started upstairs.

"I don't think," she heard her mother say as she went upstairs, "that my daughter approves of us."

For once, thought Livi, her mother appeared to have got it in one.

livi puts her foot down

L ivi spent most of Sunday playing the piano and straining her ears in the hope of hearing the telephone ring. When she was playing, she kept the soft pedal down all the time in case she didn't hear the phone.

Twice she jumped up to grab the receiver only to find the calls were for her mum. The third time it was Poppy.

"I think I've found him!" she gabbled excitedly. "This Ryan guy—he lives in a boat called . . ."

"The Pea Green Boat—I know," said Livi, relishing the fact that for once she was several steps ahead of Poppy.

"You know?" Poppy sounded deflated. "How come?"

So Livi related the whole story of The Stomping Ground and the fact that Ryan fancied her and that she reckoned they would be an item just as soon as he called her.

"If he doesn't call, I'll go and find him for you," promised Poppy. And Livi wondered whether being needed mattered to Poppy as much as having her around mattered to her friends.

"Do I get the feeling that you are expecting someone to call?" asked her mother wryly after Livi leapt up yet again from the lunch table, jettisoning carrots onto the floor in her enthusiasm to reach the phone, and looking considerably miffed when it turned out to be for Leonora.

"That guy I met at The Stomping Ground," she admitted, as Leonora burst forth in a screech of delight from the hallway phone. "Mum, he is so cool. He said he'd call me to arrange going out."

Her mother laid down her knife and fork and eyed her closely.

"So where does he come from? Is he at Bellborough?" she asked.

Livi shook her head.

"He goes to school in Kettleborough—he lives on a boat and he's got these amazing eyes . . ."

"A boat?" Her mother made it sound as if Ryan was currently living in a small box under Waterloo Bridge.

"Only in the summer," amended Livi, pulling the ring off a can of Dr Pepper. "There's nothing wrong with that."

Judy watched her daughter's eager face.

"So what's this amazing guy called?"

"Ryan—I don't know his surname."

"Oh terrific. And you think I'll let you go out with some guy whose name you don't even know?" her mother retorted, stabbing a slice of chicken with unnecessary vigour.

"Well, let me tell you, young lady, if he does ask you out—and the chances are it was all chat anyway—I shall want to meet him. You can't go dashing off with just anyone. You are only fourteen, you know, and these days you can't . . ."

Livi slammed her glass of cola on the table and slopped brown liquid over the tablecloth.

Her mother's words served only to add to the worry that had been plaguing Livi all day long. What if Ryan didn't phone?

"What is this?" she exploded. "Why can't you just be pleased for me? Just because you fouled up on your relationship, you don't want me to have one of my own, do you? You can't bear to see me happy."

Her mother shook her head.

"Oh, Livi, don't be so silly, of course I do—but you can't expect me to sanction your going out with some guy I've never met. Bring him home, and if he seems . . ."

"Oh great!" shouted Livi. "If he meets with your approval, we can go out to play. Well, tough. Because I am going out with Ryan whether you like it or not."

Her mother held up her hands, palms outwards, in a peace making gesture.

"I'm not trying to stop you," she said. "I am only concerned for your welfare—there are so many strange types around these days."

At which point, Leonora returned from her phone call carrying two bent wire coat hangers.

"Hey Judy, I've been thinking. How about after lunch I give you your first dowsing lesson?"

If we're talking strange types, thought Livi, my mother has just cornered the market.

livi takes control

When neither Adam nor Tasha turned up at school on Monday, there was much speculation about what was wrong with their mum and a great deal of murmuring about Abigail's reaction to meeting their grandmother.

"Did you phone on Sunday to find out how things were?" Tamsin asked Abigail sweetly as they changed for athletics.

Abigail shook her head.

"You should have," said Hayley accusingly. "Adam must be really upset."

"Adam's upset?" thundered Abby, flicking a strand of hair out of her eye. "How do you think I feel?"

Livi frowned. "But I didn't think you had met Adam's mum," she began.

"Not because of her, stupid," said Abigail.

CHAPTER TWENTY-TWO

"Because for six weeks, I've been going out with Adam without ever knowing he's got Indian blood in . . ."

"Abby!" Tamsin rounded on her. "For heaven's sake . . ."

"Get real, Abigail!" snapped Hayley simultaneously. "That is just so unbelievably racist."

Abigail coloured and looked away.

Livi opened her mouth to add a cutting remark, but Hayley grabbed her arm and dragged her away.

"She's not worth arguing with," she declared as they walked down the path to the games field. "But I do hope Tasha and Adam are OK. "

Livi nodded. "Me too," she agreed. "I've bought them a 'Thinking of You' card and I was going to post it. But maybe I should take it round?"

Hayley nodded enthusiastically.

"Great idea," she said. "Then you can remind them about my party on Saturday. And find out how their mum is, of course," she added hastily.

As it happened, Livi was to find out a whole lot more than that.

* * *

At break time, Livi confronted Luke Cunningham outside the music block.

"So did Mr. Golding let you off producing the concert?" she said with a grin.

Luke pulled a face.

"No chance," he said. "I told him I was a useless organiser, but he just gave me the usual bit about not knowing your strengths until you try and being certain that . . ."

"He'd found the right person? I know, I got it too." She sighed. "So I suppose we had better get started."

Luke looked anxious.

"But where do we start?" he said, taking off his glasses and wiping them on his trouser leg. "I'm seeing Poppy tonight—maybe I could pump her for ideas. I'll tell her we're stuck."

Livi bristled inwardly. OK, so Poppy was mega hot on ideas, but Livi was finally getting to the point where she didn't want anyone else telling her what to do.

"We'll put up a list and get everyone who wants to take part to sign," she said, recalling

Rosalie's advice. If the woman was going to hang around in her life, she might as well make use of her.

"We'll have a column for people who want to perform, another for those who want to help backstage and then one for people who will help with the research and writing."

Luke looked at her in admiration.

"That sounds very organised," he said, looking more cheerful. "So what's the theme?"

Livi chewed her lip.

"Have you thought of a theme?"

Livi shook her head.

"Not yet," she admitted. "Have you?"

"No," said Luke. "What if we can't think of anything?"

Livi looked at his worried features.

"Don't worry," she said cheerfully. "We will." And to her surprise, she actually found herself believing it.

tasha
opens up

At lunch time, Livi phoned home to tell her mum she would be late. After what seemed like an eternity, a breathless voice answered.

"Hello!" It was Leonora, sounding rather abrupt. "Judy Joplin's residence."

Livi cringed. She wished her mother would use her married name—it was just another sign that she was doing away with all traces of Dad.

"It's Livi," she said.

"Who?"

"Olivia," repeated Livi, praying that her 10p wouldn't run out.

"Oh sorry, dear, I was in the middle of getting Amy—that's my heroine—to see sense and the wretched child just won't pay attention. Of course, being dead always gives people ideas above their station in life," she added.

This woman, thought Livi, is seriously deranged.

"Is Mum there?" she demanded.

"No, dear, she's popped out with a couple of pixies. Oh my!" At this point there was an eruption of throaty laughter and Livi moved the receiver a few inches farther from her ear.

"What I mean is, she is out delivering. Can I take a message?"

"Just tell her I will be late home—I'm going to see a friend on the way back."

She heard the sound of a pencil scratching the message.

"OK, dear—got that. Have you ever seen a ghost?"

Livi blinked.

"Excuse me?"

"Ghosts, dear—have you . . ." She was interrupted by a series of warning bleeps on the phone.

"Must go, money running out," gabbled Livi.

"We'll discuss it later," shouted Leonora.

If my mother must have a lodger, thought

Livi, she could at least get one that was mentally stable.

Crofter's Close, where Adam and Tasha lived, was a small cul-de-sac at the bottom of Billing Hill. It wasn't until Livi was standing on the street corner, watching the bus disappear round the bend, that she realised she hadn't a clue which house it was. When she had been going out with Adam, he had never once asked her back to his house; and although he had been eager to talk a lot about the home he had left behind in Singapore, he never said a lot about his new one.

She was about to give up and post the card when she spotted a dark green Jaguar parked in the driveway of a neat little bungalow at the far end of the Close. She recognised it as the car that Adam's grandfather had been driving the previous Saturday, and summoning up her courage she marched up the path and pressed the bell.

The door opened and the same elegant woman who had met Tasha and Adam the Saturday before gazed down at her.

"Yes?" she said inclining her head.

Livi swallowed.

"I'm Livi Hunter," she said. "A friend of Tasha and Adam."

"I recognise you from Saturday." Their grandmother gave a wan smile. She looked tired and drawn. "Come—come along in."

"Thank you, Mrs . . ." Livi realised she didn't know the woman's name.

"Devi," she smiled. "Nimala Devi. Now, you'll be wanting Tasha? Adam, he is—not here."

She sighed deeply, as if the absence of her grandson was a great source of irritation to her.

She waved Livi into the back room and went to the foot of the stairs.

"Tasha? There is a friend to see you. Come, please."

Livi gazed round the room. Two huge sofas were piled with cushions in jewel shades of amethyst and jade, lavishly embroidered wall hangings depicting roaring tigers and cheerful little elephants hung from the walls and in the far corner was a wooden screen carved with tiny flowers and leaves. It was, thought Livi, one of the most beautiful rooms she had ever seen.

On the mantelpiece was a whole host of photographs, including one of a little girl sitting on the lap of a beautiful woman with waist-length black hair and a tiny, pixielike face.

"That's me and my mum." Livi turned to find Tasha looking defiantly at her.

"She's beautiful," said Livi. "You look just like her."

"Do you think so?" A faint smile crossed Tasha's lips. Livi put the photograph back and handed Tasha the card.

"I brought you this—well, it's for both of you," she amended. "From me and Hayley. We were worried—when you didn't come to school. We missed you."

Tasha looked up in surprise.

"Did you?" she said with the slightest trace of eagerness in her voice.

Livi nodded.

"Of course," she said. "How is your mum?"

"Getting better," said Tasha. "She's coming home in a couple of days."

"What was wrong with her?"

"She was just tired," said Tasha hastily, putting her card on the mantelpiece.

Livi was thinking that it was unusual to spend four days in hospital just because you were tired, when they were interrupted by Mrs. Devi bearing a large bronze tray with mugs of tea and an assortment of cakes.

"I thought," she said, putting the tray on the coffee table, "that you would enjoy a little snack."

"Wow!" said Livi in amazement. This beat a can of Coke and a Kit Kat any day.

"I hope you like them—they are Bengali delicacies; I made them to take to Ghazala—Tasha's mother—in hospital. She needs looking after."

"Dida, don't!" said Tasha, flushing bright red.

Her grandmother waved a hand dismissively.

"It is true. Remember the Hindi proverb— 'No one was ever ruined by speaking the truth,'" she said solemnly. "And now, please excuse me. I have to go and visit my poor daughter."

Tasha jumped up.

"I'll come," she said. "Please?"

167 ✳

Mrs. Devi held up her hand and shook her head.

"Not this time," she said. "Your mother will be tired. You stay, Tasha, and talk with your friend."

She paused.

"Do that, Tasha. Talk."

And with that, smiling gently at Livi, she swept out of the room.

After she had left, there was a moment's uncomfortable silence.

"Why did you really come?" asked Tasha suddenly.

Livi looked puzzled.

"What do you mean?" she said. "I came to see if you were OK and to find out about your mum."

"And the rest!" Tasha jumped to her feet, her dark eyes suddenly blazing. "Someone's said something, haven't they?"

"I don't know what you mean," protested Livi. "Said something about what?"

She wondered whether somehow Tasha had got to hear about Abigail's tirade of prejudice.

"About us—after last night, someone must have said something." Tasha's eyes filled with tears and she turned away.

Livi laid a hand gently on her shoulder.

"Some of us didn't realise that your mum was Indian, if that's what you mean," she said. "But none of us are the sort of people to care anyway." She decided against mentioning Abigail. That could wait.

"When I went out with Adam, he never said—not that there was any reason why he should . . ."

Tasha turned round.

"Adam wouldn't say," she said, biting her lip in an attempt not to cry. "He never used to be like this, but these days it's like all he wants to do is be just like Dad, completely Western. He hates it when mum or I dress traditionally. Sometimes I think he even hates me now."

A solitary tear trickled down her face. Livi wished she could think of the right thing to say.

"Of course he doesn't—you're his sister," she exclaimed. "And he is always talking about your home in Singapore, and how much he misses it and that can't be very Western."

Tasha's face crumpled.

"It's not just Singapore he misses," she said, choking back tears. "It's Dad—they used to do everything together."

Livi looked at her questioningly.

"Is he still working out there?" asked Livi. "Is that why you live with your grandparents?"

"So you don't know? No one has said anything?"

Tasha took a deep breath and looked Livi in the eye.

"I have to tell someone," she said. "My father's in prison."

Her voice faltered.

"And that's why Adam hates me. Because it's all my fault."

more
revelations

L ivi sat beside Tasha on the plush sofa, handing out tissues and listening while her friend poured her heart out.

"My dad's an antique dealer," she said. "He used to go all over the world, finding out what rich people wanted and then tracking down the right pieces for them. He's worked for lots of important families, even the Sultan of Brunei once," she added proudly.

Livi looked suitably impressed.

"Anyway, last year my dad's father died and left him quite a bit of money and Dad said he wanted to come back to England and buy an antique shop. Adam didn't seem to mind that much, but I was really fed up about it—all my friends were in Singapore and I had only been to England on holidays and it was always cold."

She nibbled a cake.

"One day, we had a terrible row," she explained. "I told him I wouldn't come, that I wanted to stay out there and that he was being selfish and cruel making me leave. He said I was being childish and didn't know what was good for me and in the end, I stormed out of the house."

She paused.

"I stayed away for ages. I know it was silly, but I thought that if I could make them see how unhappy I was, they would at least let me stay in boarding school out there and come to England in the holidays."

Livi thought she must have been pretty miserable to even contemplate such an option.

"Anyway, later that afternoon there was this massive thunderstorm, and my mum took Dad's car and came to look for me." She stopped and stared into space.

"Did she find you?" asked Livi gently.

Tasha nodded.

"But we were driving home and the rain was terrible, and suddenly the car just skidded out of control and crashed into a parked van."

"Were you hurt?" gasped Livi.

Tasha shook her head.

"Not really, just bruises and stuff, but the car was a mess and the police came and towed it away. And then a couple of days later, these men came to the house to see my dad. They said that three tiny ivory statuettes had been found hidden in the engine compartment." Tears welled in her eyes again. "They said that there were drugs inside."

"Oh, Tasha." Livi couldn't think what to say.

"They arrested my father on the spot," wept Tasha. "Just like that. He swore he knew nothing about them, but they still took him away. He's in prison out there awaiting trial and I miss him so much—and I didn't even have time to say I was sorry."

She began to cry again.

"Sorry for what?" asked Livi.

"Haven't you been listening?" snapped Tasha, brushing tears from her cheeks. "If I hadn't run off, Mum wouldn't have taken the car to look for me. And the police wouldn't have found the statuettes. And now mum is ill and it's all my fault!"

She put her head in her hands, her shoulders heaving with silent sobs.

"Stop it!" said Livi firmly, putting an arm around her. "Stop it and listen. Did *you* steal the things? Did *you* put them in the car?"

Tasha looked up in amazement.

"Of course I didn't!" she said indignantly.

"Right," said Livi. "So it isn't your fault. If your dad took them—and you don't know for sure that he did yet—that was his choice and his responsibility, not yours."

Tasha looked at her doubtfully.

A thought crossed Livi's mind.

"Was it the worry that made your mum ill?" she asked.

Tasha nodded miserably.

"It's been so horrible," she said, beginning to cry again. "My grandfather won't even let any of us mention my dad, not even Mum. He never wanted mum to marry out of her religion in the first place and now they are saying that my father has brought disgrace on the family."

She blew her nose.

"That's why Adam has turned against

everything Indian," she went on. "Neither of us really look Indian and Mum has always been happy to live in a Western way. But my grandparents are quite traditional, and now, any time Adam puts a foot wrong, they say he is just like his father and will turn out a bad lot."

"That's hardly fair!" expostulated Livi. "Adam's not the sort of person to do anything stupid."

Tasha took a deep breath.

"That's what I used to think, but now . . ." she faltered.

"Now what?" asked Livi anxiously.

"Livi, I'm scared—ever since this business with Dad, Adam's changed. It's almost like he wants to prove my grandparents right—prove that he's a loser."

"What do you mean?" asked Livi.

"That alcoholic fruit juice he was drinking on Saturday—he says it makes him feel better, stops him thinking about the trial."

Livi looked aghast.

"But how does he get it?"

Tasha hesitated.

"You won't tell?"

Livi shook her head.

"He got in with these two older guys he met at the video arcade in the holidays," she whispered. "They get it for him. But that's not all. They . . ."

She hesitated.

"Go on," said Livi.

"Well, last week they told him to take some CDs from a shop. They said if he didn't he was a wimp and they wouldn't get him any more of this stuff."

Livi gasped.

"But that's terrible!" she exclaimed. "He can't do that! Haven't you tried to stop him?"

"Of course I have!" snapped Tasha. "But he just went ahead and did it anyway. It's as if he just doesn't want to listen to reason."

Livi couldn't believe what she was hearing. Adam, the guy she had adored, being so stupid. It didn't make sense.

"He'll get caught," she said despairingly. "It's insane."

Tasha took a deep breath.

"That's why I have to help him," said Tasha, and then stopped, realising just what she had said.

Livi stared hard at her, light suddenly dawning.

"Last weekend? When I tried to see what you had been buying?" she asked.

Tasha nodded miserably.

"Adam took stuff and I said I would take it home," she said. "And now I feel so awful, so dirty."

Livi was about to protest, when a green car pulled up outside the house.

"It's my grandparents," stammered Tasha, rubbing her eyes. "You won't say anything?"

Livi shook her head.

"Not to anyone? Promise?"

Livi nodded reluctantly.

"But please, Tasha," she said, "don't get caught up with what Adam's doing—please. You promise you won't ever do that again?"

Tasha sighed.

"I won't," she said. "But I have to find a way to help Adam. After all, whatever you say, it's all my fault we're in this mess."

confusion
with connie

Livi walked home deep in thought. She wanted to help but she didn't know where to begin. If Adam was shoplifting he was bound to get caught sooner or later and that would just make everything worse for him, for his mother, for everyone. He had to be made to see sense—but she couldn't really say anything to him because Tasha had made her promise not to tell a soul.

As she turned into Billing Hill, her thoughts were diverted by the sight of a very small elderly lady in black trousers and a purple anorak, walking down the middle of the road clutching a teapot. When she spotted Livi staring at her in amazement, she waved cheerfully as if she had known her for years.

"Hello, dear," she called. "Is tea ready now?"

Livi gulped.

"I—I'm afraid I don't really know," she said, casting a glance over her shoulder to see whether there was anyone with this strange person.

"Typical!" shouted the old lady. "Rosalie said it was teatime and here I am starving to death and no one cares!"

"Rosalie?" said Livi. "You know Rosalie?" She glanced up the hill to Copperbeech. There was no sign of activity.

"Of course I do," replied the woman, waving her teapot perilously close to Livi's nose. "She's my daughter. And she never feeds me."

"Livi, I can't thank you enough!" Rosalie ran a hand distractedly through her hair. "I'd only turned my back for half a minute and she'd gone."

She pushed aside a couple of half-full packing cases, and sank down into a chair, resting her head wearily on one hand.

"She's all right now, she's watching the TV," she said, "but heaven knows where she would have ended up if you hadn't found her."

She pulled up a chair and gestured to Livi to sit down.

"She wanders off," she added unnecessarily. "She lives with Val—that's my sister—in Kettleborough, but Val's got some sort of bug so I said I'd have her for a couple of days until I start the job. Fine carer I make," she added ruefully.

Livi looked at her accusingly.

"She says you don't feed her," she declared.

Rosalie laughed.

"Poor Mum," she said. "She's just had two boiled eggs, a slice of fruit cake and three digestive biscuits for tea. I doubt she could eat another crumb if I offered it to her."

She glanced at Livi's puzzled expression.

"My mother suffers from Alzheimer's disease," she said quietly. "She forgets things. She gets confused. Sometimes she doesn't even know where she is."

Livi felt awkward. She was still trying pretty hard to hate the Wretched Rosalie, and yet she couldn't help feeling sorry for her now. She tried to imagine how she would feel if her own mum became senile, but it was so horrible she pushed the idea out of her mind.

"Your dad's out playing golf with some guy who might have some work for him," said Rosalie. "He doesn't even know about Mum being here yet. I hope he won't hit the roof."

"Of course he won't!" protested Livi. "Dad's got a really kind heart—he organised the Lions' Club Old People's lunch and did an evening a week at the night shelter and everything. Till you came along," she added snidely.

Rosalie seemed unperturbed at the dig.

"That's different," she said. "Still, we shall see. I guess it was him you were coming to see?"

Livi shook her head.

"I've been to see a friend on the way home," she said. "She's got this awful problem because her dad . . ."

She stopped. What was she at? She had sworn not to say a word to a living soul, and here she was about to confide in the one person she had vowed to hate for eternity. She was just thinking that it was odd that she had to keep reminding herself how much she hated Rosalie when the old lady shuffled into the kitchen.

"I'm Connie," she announced to Livi. "Who are you?"

"Olivia," said Livi shyly.

"*Make the babbling gossip of the air cry out 'Olivia!!'*" Connie spread her arms wide. "*Twelfth Night*, dear," she beamed, seeing Livi's astonished expression. "One of Shakespeare's better comedies, I always felt."

And with that she shuffled out of the kitchen.

Livi turned to Rosalie.

"Well, she seems pretty sane to me," she declared, deciding that Rosalie had made the whole thing up to disguise her own negligence. "Anyone who can remember Shakespeare has to be all there."

"She has her moments," said Rosalie fondly. "And then some days she doesn't even recognise her own grandchildren."

Connie reappeared at the door.

"Why won't you let me have my breakfast?" she said.

the ghost of an idea

CHAPTER TWENTY-SIX

"**I**'m back!" called Livi, dumping her bag at the bottom of the stairs.

From the back bedroom came the rattle of typewriter keys but of her mother there was no sign.

Livi ran upstairs and knocked on Leonora's door.

"Where's Mum?" she asked.

Leonora, wire-rimmed spectacles perched on the end of her nose, beamed at her.

"Olivia!" she gushed. "Just the person I need. Your mum's nipped out for some milk. Now listen, dear, I need your help. Amy is being desperately uncooperative."

Livi looked puzzled.

"Amy, dear—she's my heroine; fifteen years old, a terrible know-all and dead," Leonora explained briskly. "What used to be her family home is now a Youth Centre and she keeps trying to come back and sort out the lives of the modern day kids. What I need to know from you is this: how many of your friends actually believe in ghosts?

Livi stared at her.

"Livi, dear?" encouraged Leonora.

"That's it," breathed Livi. "That is very definitely it!"

"Excuse me?"

"Ghosts," repeated Livi. "For the concert. The ghosts of the first pupils coming back to watch us. Leonora, you are brilliant!"

And she gave her a spontaneous hug. And then remembered that this was the woman who was rapidly leading her mother astray.

"I'm not sure what I've said," beamed Leonora, "but I'm pleased it helped. Now, about these ghosts . . ."

* * *

"Where's Leonora?" asked Judy when she returned with the milk.

"She said she was going to see her sister to blow the cobwebs away," grinned Livi. "She's quite cool when you get to know her."

Judy raised an eyebrow.

"Praise indeed, coming from you," she laughed. "I don't suppose Dad dropped by?"

Livi shook her head.

"Typical," said her mother. "He said he'd bring the promised cheque, but then knowing him it won't materialise. I suppose he expects me to tell the gas board and Barclaycard to sing for their money."

She closed her eyes momentarily and yawned. Livi thought how tired she looked.

"Mum?" she said.

"Mmm?"

"I do love you," said Livi, giving her a big hug.

Judy looked inordinately pleased.

"What brought that on?" she said, hugging Livi back.

Livi shrugged. She didn't want to say that although her mum was totally off the wall, it was good to have someone to feel safe with.

"Oh, no reason," she said. "Did you know that Rosalie's mother has Alzheimer's disease?"

Judy raised an eyebrow.

"No, who told you that?"

"I found her wandering down Billing Hill," said Livi and proceeded to tell her mother the story of Connie.

Her mother looked thoughtful.

"And she lives with them?" she asked disbelievingly.

Livi shook her head.

"I think she's just staying for a day or two," she said. "Till Rosalie's sister gets better."

Judy looked thoughtful.

"Let's hope for Rosalie's sake, she gets better soon," she said wryly. "I can't see your dear father wanting that situation to go on for long."

"What's for supper?" asked Livi in a desperate bid to stop her mother relaunching a verbal attack on her dad's faults and failings.

"Cannelloni," said her mother. "Hungry?"

"Starved," said Livi. "And shattered. I don't intend to do a single thing tonight except eat and phone Poppy and watch TV."

"Oh dear," said her mother, pursing her lips. "That could be awkward."

"What do you mean? I did my homework in

my study period, if that's what you're worried about—and I'll practise the oboe tomorrow morning. I've no puff left in me."

Her mother smiled.

"Oh, it's not that," she said. "Only this guy—Ryan, is it?—he phoned and said he'd be calling round later."

Livi leapt out of her chair.

"He did? When? What time? Why didn't you tell me?"

"I just have," retorted her mother rationally. "And don't get in a flap; he won't be here for at least half an hour."

"Half an hour!" screeched Livi. "Oh my God—my hair. It's a mess! I'll never get it dry in time."

She made a dash for the door.

"Hold your horses!" protested her mother, removing a dish from the oven. "What about the cannelloni?"

"Stuff the cannelloni!" snapped Livi.

"I already did," said her mother dryly, taking her by the shoulders and plonking her down at the kitchen table. "Eat!"

mothers!

Ten minutes later, hiccupping violently as a result of having eaten her supper in record time, Livi was standing in front of her wardrobe in her bra and pants, hair dripping onto her shoulders, agonising over what to wear. Suddenly every garment looked dated and boring. She couldn't wear the dress he'd seen on Saturday and her mother, in what Livi deemed to be great dereliction of maternal duty, had failed to wash either her Lycra leggings or her silk shirt.

She was weighing up the merits of her lime green mini-skirt against her lilac hipsters when the doorbell rang.

"You must be Ryan," she heard her mother trill. "Come through to the kitchen; Livi's still tied up in the beauty regime!"

Livi cringed. Her mother was such a total embarrassment. Didn't she realise that you never, ever let a guy think you had made an effort? They were supposed to assume that you always looked stunning.

"Now do tell me about yourself!" Judy Hunter's voice floated up the stairs and Livi heard the kitchen door shut.

Throwing on her orange cropped top and lilac skirt, and spraying herself rather too liberally with Anais Anais, she belted for the stairs. If it was a choice between the full make-up and leaving Ryan to the mercies of her mother, she would just have to hope he was the sort of guy who went for the bare-faced look.

"Hi," said Ryan as she burst into the kitchen. "You look great."

Livi smiled what she hoped was a seductive smile and prayed that Ryan couldn't see how violently her heart was thumping in her chest.

"Coffee?" said her mother.

"No, Mum, we'll just . . ." began Livi, desperate to prevent her mother from conducting her usual investigative interview reserved for new boyfriends.

"That would be great," said Ryan, smiling charmingly. He winked at Livi. "And then maybe you wouldn't mind if Livi and I went for a walk?"

A thrill of anticipation cantered down Livi's spine.

Her mother looked doubtful. If you dare say no, thought Livi, I am leaving home.

"Well, I suppose for a short while," said Judy.

Livi breathed an inward sigh of relief. It was going to be all right. Her mother was going to behave.

She should have known better than to make snap judgements.

During the course of one mug of coffee, Judy managed to enquire about Ryan's schooling, his mother's career, and his aspirations for the future. Livi thought she would die of embarrassment.

Ryan, however, seemed unperturbed.

"You must meet my mum," he said. "You'd have a lot in common—she's a painter and illustrator. In fact," he added as if the idea had just struck him, "she's showing at an exhibition at the Adnitt Gallery in a couple of weeks time. I could get you tickets."

Judy's eyes lit up.

"Could you really?" she enthused. "That would be marvellous."

"I'll drop a couple in for you and Mr. Hunter," said Ryan.

"Just one will be fine," said Judy shortly.

Ryan paused.

"Mr. Hunter isn't keen on art?" he asked casually.

"Not as keen as he is on other things," she retorted and Livi's heart lurched. Please God, don't let her say anything awful. "Mike doesn't live here anymore."

"Mike?" said Ryan. "Your husband's name is Mike?"

Judy nodded, a puzzled look on her face.

"Oh, it's nothing—just that my dad was called Mike," said Ryan hastily. "He died."

Judy looked sympathetic.

"I'm so sorry," she said. "No, Mike has decided that the decent husband and father bit isn't for him and . . ."

"Mum!" hissed Livi under her breath. "Come on, Ryan, let's go."

Ryan stood up.

"So Mr. Hunter doesn't live round here?" he asked, looking, Livi thought, unnecessarily perturbed at the news. It was one thing to win the parents over, but this was going way over the top.

"Oh yes!" snapped Judy. "He has taken it upon himself to set up home with his—his new partner—on our doorstep." She caught Livi's infuriated gaze and looked slightly sheepish.

"Anyway, you don't want to listen to me going on," she said, assuming a false brightness.

No, thought Livi, we don't.

"Let's go," she said to Ryan, before her mother could find something else derogatory to say about her dad. As if Ryan cared about their domestic hiccups.

Had Livi realised just how much he cared, she would have had even greater cause for concern.

"This is it," said Ryan, gesturing to a red and green painted narrowboat moored alongside the towpath. "Welcome to The Pea Green Boat!"

"It's lovely," enthused Livi, enchanted by the painted flowerpots on the cabin roof and the little ruched curtains at the windows.

"Mum," he said to a thin woman with hair scraped back into a ballerina-style bun, who was sitting at an easel on the towpath painting in the warm evening sunshine. "This is Olivia—the girl I was telling you about."

Ryan's mother raised her eyes, looked at Livi and opened her mouth.

And shut it again. And blinked.

"Hello," said Livi nervously.

With a small shake of the head, his mum put her paintbrush to one side and stood up.

"My dear, how are you?" she said softly. Her eyes scanned Livi's face intently, until she began to feel quite uncomfortable.

"Fine, thank you, Mrs. . . ."

"Oh call me Cordy, everyone else does," said his mum.

That name rings a bell, thought Livi, but couldn't think why.

"We're going for a walk," announced Ryan. "See you later."

His mother held up her hand.

"Wait," she said. "You bring a charming friend back to meet me and then don't give me a chance to get to know her. Have a drink before you go."

"OK, but we'll only stay a minute," agreed Ryan uncomfortably.

They climbed through the narrow doorway into the cabin and Cordy opened a small fridge and took out a bottle of white wine and two cans of Seven Up.

"So have you lived in Leehampton all your life?" she asked, smiling at Livi as she poured out drinks. "Are you at school locally?"

Livi nodded, wondering what it was with adults that necessitated their having a potted biography of everyone they met.

"That's nice," she said. "When Gerald was alive we moved around so much, I never felt we had roots. I grew up in Hunstanton," she added looking straight at Livi. "I miss the sea."

"Really?" said Livi. "That's where my dad used to live—my gran still does."

Ryan put his glass on the table and stood up hastily.

"We're going for a walk," he said. "See you later."

His mother looked at him, her face very serious.

"All right," she said at last. "But Ryan . . ."

"What now?" he said impatiently.

"Be careful."

Ryan looked embarrassed.

"Mothers!" he said to Livi with a grin.

"Tell me about it," said Livi, cringing as she recalled her mother's unforgivable outburst.

It wasn't until much later that night, as she lay wide awake reliving every moment of her evening with Ryan, that it occurred to Livi that he had told her mum that his dad was called Mike. Only his mother had said it was Gerald.

Not that it mattered one way or the other, she thought sleepily. It was only a name after all. And the poor guy was dead anyway.

heights and depths

Over the next two weeks, Livi lurched between a state of blissful happiness and periods of intense panic. Ryan phoned her nearly every evening and was always turning up on the doorstep to see her. Her mother, who would normally have thrown a blue fit at the idea of Livi shirking The Causes and Effects of the French Revolution in favour of love, was prevented from creating too much of a scene by what Livi saw as a most convenient stroke of fate.

One evening, she stuck her head round the sitting room door to find her mother and Leonora in the most contorted positions murmuring to themselves to a background of *Sounds of the Rain Forest*.

"Mum, Ryan's coming round—that is OK, isn't it?" she said, wondering what it would be like to have a normal mother.

Judy unwrapped her left leg from her right shoulder and looked dubious.

"Have you done your . . ."

"Yes, I've done the essay, practised the oboe, and ironed my shirt," recited Livi. "So can he?"

Livi didn't mention that he was already on his way.

"Only for an hour," said her mother firmly. "Ryan or no Ryan, you need your sleep."

Livi stuck out her tongue and grinned.

"This Ryan?" enquired Leonora, not opening her eyes. "Boyfriend?"

"Yes," said Livi shortly, irritated at Leonora's inquisitiveness but chuffed at being able to say she had a boyfriend.

"Lives on a boat, apparently," said Judy, in slightly sceptical tones.

Leonora's eyes flew open.

"So it is my Ryan!" gasped Leonora. "Cordy's boy—well I never did!" She clapped her hands together in glee. "I told you about my sister—the illustrator. Spends the summer on this old narrowboat. It's down by the lock," she added.

That's where I heard the name, thought Livi in surprise.

"So Ryan is your nephew?" she said incredulously.

Leonora nodded.

"Isn't that just the neatest thing?" she enthused just as the doorbell rang.

Livi ran to let Ryan in.

"We've got your aunt here!" she said accusingly, as if he should have informed her of this family connection.

Ryan's eyes widened as Livi led him through to the sitting room.

"Auntie Leo? What are you doing here?" he asked.

"These are my lodgings," she said. "I told you both—remember? All about darling Judy and the cute little house and all."

Ryan frowned.

"I thought you said you were staying with the Joplins, or some such? I hadn't a clue you were here, at Livi's," he added, looking rather concerned.

"Oh, I work under my maiden name," said

Judy. "That'll be why." She turned to Leonora. "My married name is Hunter."

Leonora cocked her head on one side and looked thoughtful.

"Hunter," she said. "That name rings a bell—now who did I know called Hunter?"

Ryan suddenly burst in enthusiastically.

"Well, don't let us interrupt you any longer," he said. "Come on Livi, let's go."

"He's a nice boy, Judy, very reliable," Livi heard Leonora say as she shut the sitting room door. Livi could have hugged her. She might be leading her mother astray drinking red wine and trying out a whole host of weird alternative therapies, with the result that the sitting room smelt of bergamot oil and the milk saucepan was encrusted with strange green deposits, which Leonora ensured her was the residue of their attempt to make Wood Betony and Linden tea. But if she was responsible for encouraging her mother to let her out midweek, Livi was prepared to turn a blind eye to her eccentricities.

"Oh, I am pleased," Livi heard her mother say as Ryan opened the front door. "Now I know he's your nephew, there's no problem about Livi seeing as much of him as she likes."

But the problem was waiting quite quietly just around the corner.

livi has
high hopes

While Livi decided to overlook the extraordinary behaviour of her mum and Leonora, there were a number of things that she could not so easily ignore. Ryan, for all his attentiveness, had not kissed her. Not properly. He brushed his lips across her forehead occasionally, but every time it seemed as though he was about to get really passionate, he had second thoughts and stopped. Livi had tried everything; she cleaned her teeth every hour, sucked breath fresheners, sprayed herself with Anais Anais—but nothing worked. She couldn't ask any of her friends what she was doing wrong, because that would be to admit that she obviously wasn't even a little bit sexy.

She thought about asking her mum—but then reckoned it was too risky. If Judy went all maternal and got visions of her daughter in a passionate embrace, she might put a stop to Ryan's visits and Livi couldn't bear that.

She bet Rosalie knew all the tricks, she thought to herself. Not, of course, that Livi would resort to the sort of cheap ploys that Rosalie must have used to snare her innocent father. And anyway, Livi had every reason to believe that God had paid attention to her prayers and that her father was beginning to pine quite seriously for her mum.

Three times that week she had got home from school to find her dad sitting at the kitchen table, hands wrapped round a mug of coffee chatting to her mum. The first time the conversation was pretty heated, but Livi noticed with great satisfaction that by the third visit, her mother had put cheese and biscuits on the table and was laughing at one of her dad's jokes.

"This is nice," he had purred with satisfaction the evening before. "Just like old times." And Livi had noticed that her mother didn't say anything remotely sarcastic, but merely asked him if he would like a glass of wine.

If things went on like this, it couldn't be long before Dad was home for good. And if she could just get Ryan to profess his undying love, life would be absolutely perfect.

But perfection, as everyone finds out sooner or later, is in very short supply.

revealing
research

The concert was only a couple of weeks away, but Livi was discovering that now she had Ryan and things with dad were looking up, she was actually beginning to enjoy her role of producer.

The ghost idea went down a storm. Everyone suddenly got very enthusiastic, rushing around snatching net curtains from their parents' bedroom windows to make themselves look suitably wraith-like and making echo boxes to increase the funereal quality of their voices. Luke wrote some ethereal music and Mr. Ostler, who was head of music and looked like a rather agitated chipmunk, organised the choir into some very sepulchral choral work. Livi, for the first time in her life, found herself telling other people what to do.

"Mia, you are supposed to be dying of

consumption," she said at rehearsal one afternoon. "Couldn't you look a bit more wan? And Hayley, you're a ghost whose never seen a computer room before—please look at least a little bewildered!"

Livi's one failure had been in getting Tasha or Adam to take part. Tasha said she was too shy to act and Adam said it was all stupid anyway and why should he bother?

"You could be Sir Ambrose," she said, hoping that the offer of this dramatic gem would make him change his mind. "Everyone has to do something—Gee-Gee's golden rule!"

"I'll paint scenery," he said grudgingly and stomped off in a huff.

"Livi, how do I look?" asked Tamsin, who had managed to get her own way and was playing the part of Lady Lavinia, Sir Ambrose's wife. She twirled around in an empire line dress left over from Year Ten's production of *Northanger Abbey*.

"Fine," said Livi distractedly.

"No, that's not right." Tasha came over from the corner where she had been sitting acting as prompt. "That sash is quite the wrong colour for the dress. Look, this is better," and she snatched up a lavender sash from the costume box.

The whole dress looked different.

"Wow!" said Tamsin in admiration. "That's cool! Thanks, Tasha."

Livi recalled how Tasha had instinctively known what would suit her when they were in Togs 'n' Clogs together.

"Can you take charge of the costumes for the orphans and ghosts?" pleaded Livi. "And think of something for Sir Ambrose to wear? You're so good at it."

Tasha paused.

"OK, then," she said. "I'd like that. Except I don't know what people wore in England back then," she said.

"No problem," said Livi, remembering Rosalie's offer. "Leave it to me."

The following afternoon, on the way home from school, she called at Copperbeech, hoping that Rosalie had some books on costume.

She heard the raised voices as she turned into the driveway.

"Isn't that just typical!" Rosalie's voice

shrilled through the open window. "Here I am, working all hours, and I ask one small favour . . ."

"One small favour! Tying myself to the house and a loony old woman all day? I've better things to do."

"Like what? Waiting for these wonderful jobs to fall into your lap? Spending hours around the golf course? Wasting your redundancy money?"

Livi stood speechless in the porch. Should she ring the bell? Or go away and pretend she hadn't heard anything.

"But I want it to be just the two of us," Mike said. "Like it used to be. Can't your mother go into a home? Just till your sister's better?"

Her father's voice was pleading now.

"No, she can't!" snapped Rosalie. "You were the one who wanted the big house, so that everyone would think how well you were doing. Well, now we *have* got the space, we're going to have Mum here!"

"Oh, are we?" shouted Mike. "If I'd wanted to drown in a sea of domestic drudgery, I could have stayed at home."

"Then why didn't you?" Rosalie's voice

sounded more tearful now. "If what I am suggesting is so awful, why don't you go back home to Judy."

"I might just do that!" roared her father, and with that, a door slammed and Livi could hear no more.

She turned and went down the path. It sounded as if her dad and Rosalie really were falling out, and he was thinking of coming home. Then Rosalie would get what she deserved. Livi wondered why she didn't feel more comfortable about it.

party
pooper

Hayley's party was the first one that Livi had really enjoyed since Poppy's sister had her eighteenth, despite the fact that Poppy wasn't there, but tucked up in bed with tonsillitis. And it was all down to Ryan. Being with the guy that everyone else fancied was a real morale booster and Livi found herself making jokes and talking about everything from gun control to soul and rap without once worrying about whether she sounded stupid or whether her concealer was doing a good enough job of hiding her freckles. Her greatest source of satisfaction was the look of blatant envy on Abigail's face. Having dumped Adam the week before, she was on her own, which Livi reckoned was something of a new experience for her.

Halfway through the evening, Hayley grabbed Ryan by the arm.

"Hey," she said, "come and dance with me. You have to—everyone has to dance with the birthday girl!"

Ryan laughed.

"OK, OK," he said, letting himself be dragged away. "Back in a minute," he mouthed to Livi.

Livi was just helping herself to another glass of fruit punch when someone came up behind her and put their hands over her eyes.

"Agh!" Livi spilt her glass of punch all down the front of her dress. She wheeled round.

"Adam!" He was standing there, his indigo eyes unusually bright, with a silly grin on his face.

"That's me!" he said. "Come and dance."

"No way," said Livi in disgust. "You've been drinking.

"*'You've been drinking!'*" mimicked Adam. "Of course I have—what else do people do at parties?"

Tasha, who had been sitting at the bottom of the stairs talking to Mia, came through to get a drink. She took one look at her brother's glazed expression and exploded.

"Adam! Are you mad? You said you weren't

going to drink any more of that stuff!" She glanced round the kitchen. "Where is it?"

"All gone," beamed Adam. "Shame," he added mournfully.

"You're totally out of it, aren't you?" yelled Tasha.

A small crowd had gathered at the kitchen door, alerted by the commotion. "You being like this isn't going to help anything. Mum's in hospital, Dad's in prison, and now you . . ."

She stopped, aghast at what she had said.

"Prison?" someone in the doorway whispered.

"Shut up!" roared Adam. "Now look what you've done. Now everyone knows!"

Shoving his sister out of the way, he pushed through the group into the hallway and out of the front door. Tasha burst into tears.

Everyone was standing around looking a bit awkward and not knowing what to do. From the darkened lounge, Smashing Pumpkins thundered from the stereo. In the kitchen, people started murmuring.

"Those sort of people are like that," Livi heard Abigail mutter.

"What's he in prison for?" someone else whispered.

"He was drunk!"

Livi decided enough was enough.

"Look after Tasha," she told Tamsin. "I'll go and sort Adam."

"Better?" Livi handed Adam her handkerchief.

She had found him throwing up noisily and unattractively into a flower bed.

When he had finished, Livi saw that he was also crying.

"Look," she said, sitting down on the grass beside him. "I know all about your dad."

"Tasha told you," Adam remarked dully, wiping his mouth with the handkerchief.

"Yes, she did," admitted Livi. "She is very worried about you. It's just not fair, Adam."

"I know," he said eagerly. "Dad's innocent, I know he is."

"I didn't mean that," interrupted Livi. "The way you are behaving isn't fair. Not to Tasha, or your mum, or your dad."

Adam stared at her.

"What do you mean?" he mumbled.

"Your dad might be innocent and he's hanging in there, holding on to the thought that you are all rooting for him and supporting each other," she said. "Instead of that, you're wallowing in self-pity . . ."

"I'm not," Adam began to protest.

"Oh yes you are!" retorted Livi. "Drinking because it makes you feel good without thinking about how it makes other people feel, taking stuff, putting your sister at risk. You're disgusting," she added to emphasise her point.

Adam was silent.

"Look," said Livi more gently. "You don't need all this. You've got us—all your friends. We're behind you."

"Oh yes?" said Adam sarcastically. "Abby couldn't get away quick enough."

"That was nothing to do with your dad, and you know it," said Livi practically. "Abigail is a prejudiced, narrow-minded bigot. There are plenty of much nicer girls around."

Adam burped.

"But frankly, while you're in this mess, any

girl with half a brain would steer well clear," she added acerbically.

Adam looked sheepish and Livi noticed that he was turning rather green again.

"I don't even like the stuff much," he said. "It just helps me to stop thinking about Dad all those miles away waiting for the trial . . ."

"Being with your friends works just as well," said Livi. "And it's a whole lot better for your liver."

Adam gave a small smile.

"It's been not having anyone to talk to that's the worst," he said. "My grandfather is so anti my father there isn't any point, and I felt like if I told anyone else, it would be betraying my dad."

"You can talk to me any time," avowed Livi.

"I can? I mean, I thought you and that Ryan guy . . ."

"So I'm going out with Ryan? That doesn't stop us being friends, does it?"

Adam didn't reply. He was being sick all over a small laurel bush. Livi thought that there was nothing less sexy or attractive than a guy throwing up.

"Sorry," he said.

"Promise you won't touch that stuff ever again?" demanded Livi. "It doesn't solve a thing."

"I know," said Adam. "And the way I feel right now, I never want to drink again." He took a deep breath.

"I'd better go back and find Tasha," he said. "I've been pretty foul to her lately. She probably hates me."

Livi shook her head.

"Of course she doesn't," she said. "She thinks you hate *her*."

Adam's eyes widened in surprise.

"I don't hate her," he said. "I blamed her at first, but that was just because I needed someone to blame. But I don't hate her—she's my sister."

"Then why don't you go and tell her that?" suggested Livi.

a big shock
for livi

"So I really think it won't be long before Dad comes back," Livi told Ryan on Sunday afternoon as they walked back from the canal.

She had got home from the party to find her parents in the sitting room, drinking coffee.

" . . . so you see, it simply won't work out," she heard her father say as she went into the room. "I want you both, I . . ." He had stopped when he saw Livi, but she was certain that any day now that tight-lipped look on her mum's face would give way to ecstatic joy. Dad wanted them both and everything would be all right.

"That's great," agreed Ryan. "So when can I meet him? I'd really like to—you know, to talk music and stuff," he added hastily. "Maybe he'd lend me some of his Elvis music."

After her mother's embarrassing outburst, Livi had been very reluctant to allow Ryan near either of her parents for fear of what they might say or do, but with things looking so much better, she thought she could probably risk it.

"OK," she said, slipping her hand into his and smiling up at him. "What's it worth?"

Ryan stopped and leaned towards her. Livi held her breath. He gave her a big hug. It was nice, but it wasn't what she wanted.

As they turned the corner into Silverdale Road, Livi saw her father's car parked outside her house.

"He's there again!" she declared with the utmost satisfaction. "So you can meet him now."

Ryan suddenly looked apprehensive.

"You sure it will be all right?" he asked nervously. "I mean, your mum won't mind?"

Livi shook her head.

"'Course not," she averred. "She likes you."

Her father was in the kitchen, leaning against the Welsh dresser and Livi almost burst with joy to note that his hand was resting lightly at Judy's back—and she hadn't shrugged it away.

"You're back early," commented her mother, and Livi hoped that meant she wanted more time alone with her father.

"We're not stopping," she assured her hastily.

"Livi! How are you, sweetheart!" exclaimed her father. "And this is . . ."

"Dad, this is Ryan," said Livi.

Her father put out his hand and shook Ryan's vigorously.

"Good to meet you," he said. "You're the guitar player?"

Ryan nodded, not taking his eyes off Mike's face.

"I strum a little myself," said Mike, easing himself into a chair and picking up his coffee. "Have done for years."

For the next ten minutes, Mike and Ryan talked about guitars and Mike promised to look out his old sheet music and pass it on via Livi.

"Tell you what," he said. "Why don't I nip back for my guitar and we'll have a bit of a session?"

No, pleaded Livi silently.

"Great!" said Ryan.

"Well actually, I was . . ." began Judy.

"Won't take long," said Mike enthusiastically. "I'll be back in ten minutes."

I knew that introducing Ryan to Dad would lead to trouble, she thought.

Quite how much she was about to find out.

ryan drops a bombshell

While her father was driving across Leehampton, Livi and Ryan were sitting on the end of her bed listening to her *Hang Out* CD. Ryan was unusually quiet and replied to Livi's questions in monosyllables. Perhaps, thought Livi, he was shy and trying to pluck up courage to kiss her. In which case, it would be only reasonable for her to make it easier for him.

It was, thought Livi, now or never.

"I really like you," she said, running her fingers through the waves of hair at the nape of his neck.

Ryan turned and smiled gently at her.

"And I like you too," he said.

He cupped her face gently in his hands and pulled her towards him.

CHAPTER THIRTY-THREE

This is it, she thought ecstatically. He's going to kiss me. I think I might die.

He leaned towards her and his lips brushed hers, lingering uncertainly for a long moment. Then suddenly, he dropped his hands and turned away.

"We mustn't," he said. "I'm sorry. Really, I am sorry."

Livi felt a surge of disappointment.

"What's wrong? What have I done?" she said.

Ryan walked over to the window, his hands in his pockets.

"I don't think we should see one another like this anymore," he said.

Livi's stomach churned and she felt sick. He couldn't mean it. Not Ryan. They had been getting on so well.

"Why?" she cried. "What have I done? I thought you cared; you said you really liked me."

Ryan turned back and faced her, his face slightly flushed. He reached out and touched her shoulder.

"Oh Livi, I do like you. I like you a lot," he said.

"Why then?" Livi pleaded. "Give me one good reason why!"

Ryan took a deep breath.

"Because," he said, with a tinge of regret in his voice, "because I think you are my sister."

Livi felt as if someone had kicked her in the stomach. His sister? What was he talking about?

Somewhere in the distance she heard the front door slam and her father's voice calling to her mum.

"What do you mean?" she stammered. "How can I be your sister?"

Ryan turned and looked at her.

"I think that your dad is my dad, too," he said, dropping his eyes. "I'm almost certain."

Livi felt like Alice trapped in the nonsense world of Wonderland.

"But your dad is dead—you told me so," she protested.

Ryan sat on the bed.

"The guy I always called Dad—believed was my dad, was really my stepfather," he explained.

"It wasn't until after he died that Mum told me. And then only because she had no choice," he added rather bitterly.

Livi felt as if she were drowning.

"He left me some money," said Ryan. "And in his will it said 'for Ryan, whom I loved as if he were my own.'" He brushed a hand across his face and Livi saw that there were tears in his eyes. She reached a hand out to him and then pulled back. Suddenly she didn't know the rules anymore.

"I asked Mum and she told me. She said she'd been in love with a guy called Mike Hunter, but that he had fallen for someone else and had gone off to live in the Midlands. A month after he left, she found out she was pregnant."

Livi swallowed.

"You?" she whispered.

Ryan nodded.

"So you see," he said. "We can't go on like this. It wouldn't be right. You're my half sister."

The words hit Livi like a bullet.

"It's all stupid!" she said bursting into tears. "It can't be true. Your mum would have written to my dad and told him about you if it was true. You've made it up!"

Ryan shook his head.

"I wish," he said, "that I had. I thought I wanted to find my real father, but if it means giving you up . . ."

He stood up.

"Come downstairs with me," he pleaded. "And let's get this sorted out once and for all."

"Well, there you are," cried Mike as Livi and Ryan walked into the kitchen.

"Livi?" asked Judy, seeing her daughter's grim expression. "What's wrong? Have you two had a row?"

She glared at Ryan.

"Oh Mum, it's . . ." Livi fell into Judy's arms and sobbed.

"What's going on?" enquired Mike, looking bewildered.

"I think," said Ryan, "I can explain."

"Explain!" ordered Judy, still holding the sobbing Livi.

Ryan turned to Mike.

"I believe," he said, "you know my mother. Cordelia French. Only when you knew her, she was Cordelia Carstairs."

"Yes," Mike said slowly. "Yes, I do. It was a long time ago."

Ryan looked him straight in the eye.

"Seventeen years ago, I think you will find," he said softly.

Livi felt her mother's arms drop away from holding her. She raised a tear-stained face to see a horrified look of recognition cross her face. She stood, motionless, staring at her husband.

For a moment, Mike sat completely still. He looked at Ryan and Ryan looked back at him. The clock on the wall ticked importantly. The cold water tap, which Judy had been meaning to fix for weeks, dripped rhythmically.

It was, thought Livi, as if someone had pressed the freeze-frame button on a video.

Suddenly, the silence was broken by Leonora bursting through the kitchen door, dressed in a scarlet cape and enormous fur hat and looking as if she had just escaped from the Red Army.

"Hi, people!" she said, slamming two bottles of champagne onto the table. "Celebration time—the book's finished." She paused. "Oh, I'm sorry, Judy. I didn't realise you had company . . ."

She stopped, staring at Mike.

"Great Scott," she breathed. "Michael Hunter. What the hell are you doing here?"

"Mike," said Judy, in a tight, clipped voice, "is my husband. Olivia's father."

Leonora looked at Mike and then at Ryan. She took in Livi's tear-stained face and Judy's tense posture.

"This," she said, with magnificent understatement, "is a bit of a dilemma."

It seemed to Livi that from that moment, Leonora took charge. She swept out into the hall, made a brief phone call and then insisted that everyone sat down around the kitchen table while she made tea and cut huge wedges of fruit loaf. No one ate a mouthful; they simply picked at it, Livi sniffing quietly and Mike drumming his fingers self-consciously on the back of the chair.

"So you're my son?" Mike breathed the words in disbelief.

Ryan nodded, scanning Mike's face for his reaction.

"I don't understand," he said. "I never realised—I mean, when your mother and I broke up, I had no idea."

"And would it have made any difference if you had?" Judy's voice was tight with emotion.

Mike ran his fingers through his hair.

"I . . ." he began, but was interrupted by the sound of the doorbell.

"That," said Leonora, wiping her hands on a tea towel, "will be my sister."

Ryan's mother took Judy's hand in both of hers.

"Please believe me," she said, "I would not have had this happen for all the world." She turned to Livi's father.

"Mike—I'm sorry."

"I didn't have any idea—why didn't you tell me?"

Cordelia smiled ruefully.

"What would have been the point?" she said.

"You had already left—you told me you loved Judy to distraction and couldn't bear not to be with her. Do you honestly think I would come crawling to you, knowing that?"

She turned to Livi.

"My dear, this must be awful for you—I knew the moment Ryan brought you down to the boat that you were Mike's daughter—you are so like him."

Livi turned on Ryan, all her pent-up misery spilling out.

"You used me!" she shouted. "You chatted me up and made me think you liked me, and all because you thought that you could get to my dad through me. How could you? How could you do that?"

Ryan's cheek burned scarlet.

"It wasn't like that, Livi, you have to believe me," he pleaded. "I really do like you and at first, I guessed it was just a coincidence about your surname being Hunter. And then when your mum said that her husband was called Mike . . ."

"You said that your dad was called Mike and that he had died!" snapped Livi.

"I know, I lied," admitted Ryan. "I still wasn't sure, and anyway I had to cover up my surprise from your mum." He turned to Judy. "I'm sorry," he added. "Maybe I should just have kept quiet."

Judy touched his arm.

"No," she said quietly. "This has all been hushed up for too long. We shall just have to deal with it as best we can."

She looked at Livi with a gentle smile.

"You always said you wished you had a brother," she said. "Well, now you have."

coming to
terms

"**Y**ou mean, Ryan is your brother?" Hayley said incredulously after Livi had poured out the story the next day at school.

"Half-brother," she corrected.

"That means you can't go out with him," maintained Abigail, tossing her head. "Which leaves him free for me, doesn't it?"

"Oh shut up, Abigail Lane!" shouted Tasha. "Can't you see Livi's upset? Have you no feelings?"

Abigail blushed and said nothing. The rest of the gang were rendered speechless. Tasha was normally such a mouse. To hear her leaping to Livi's defence was a totally new experience.

Livi shot her a grateful glance.

"Look on the bright side!" encouraged Hayley, who was always determined to get the best out of any situation. "You could write about it and sell your story to *Lovelines*. You know their Love Crisis slot—it pays £100!"

Livi's eyes widened.

"It does?" she said. "No, no I couldn't do it."

Her life was as good as over. She had to start thinking of Ryan as a brother and not a boyfriend and would probably never, ever fall in love again. Her pain was too deep to talk about, let alone commit to print.

On the other hand, £100 was a lot of money.

She started the story that evening, sitting at the kitchen table. After twenty minutes of scribbling and crossing out, and sniffing at the sad bits, she was about to give up.

"How on earth do you do a whole book?" she asked Leonora, who was brewing some foul-smelling concoction that she assured Livi would whiten her skin. "I can't even get the first paragraph right."

Leonora laughed.

"It's blood, sweat and tears, dear," she said. "I always think it's worse than giving birth. The conception is great fun, but getting it into the world hurts like hell!" She stirred the saucepan vigorously and sniffed the contents.

"I have been known to throw pot plants out of the window when things get really bad," she commented. "What are you trying to do?"

Livi told her about the £100.

"I thought it might help," said Livi. "You know, get things clear in my mind."

"A very good idea," agreed Leonora. "Want some help?"

Livi nodded eagerly.

"And Livi," she said, "I am sorry I didn't realise sooner. About Ryan and you. I could have saved you so much pain."

Livi smiled.

"Well, at least there's one good thing about it," she said.

"What's that?" asked Leonora.

"At least this time I was dumped for a good reason."

They both laughed and Livi realised that although she was going to take a long time to get over all this, one day she would.

good news for judy, bad news for livi

few days later, Livi got home from school to find Ryan's mother sitting at the table drinking coffee with her mum. She felt very awkward, not really knowing what to say and wondering why Cordelia should be holding what appeared to be an animated conversation with her mother.

"Hi, there, Livi!" Her mum seemed unusually cheerful. "Wonderful news!"

Livi waited.

"Cordelia thinks that my pieces are exceptional!" she said.

"Pieces?" said Livi.

"My gnomes, darling, and the leprechaun and the elves."

"Oh, and I particularly enjoyed the worried witches," interjected Cordelia, patting her bun into place. "When I saw them in the hall last weekend I was so excited, but it hardly seemed the time or the place to discuss commissions," she added dryly.

Judy jumped up to refill the coffee pot.

"Cordelia has a shareholding in The Potting Shed," her mum enthused.

Livi looked blank.

"It's a really upmarket craft shop in Fulham," she said. "And they are going to take a dozen of my things and see if they sell. And if they do . . ." She paused as if carried away by the sheer enormity of the possibilities.

"If they do, and they will," declared Cordelia, "a Judy Joplin fairyland piece could be the essential accessory in Knightsbridge homes by Christmas!"

"Isn't it exciting!" Livi had temporarily forgotten her misery, so impressed was she at the thought of her mother's gnomes and goblins holding court in the hallways of the rich and famous. "You'll make a fortune."

And I might get to wear decent gear at last, she thought.

"It is fun, isn't it?" agreed her mother. "And financially, it couldn't have come at a better time."

"Dad said he'd . . ." began Livi.

"Sit down a minute, sweetheart," said her mother. "There's something I have to tell you."

"I've got to finish my geography project work or old Peewit will go ballistic," said Livi. "Is it important?"

"It is rather," said her mother and took a deep breath.

"Your father and I . . ." she paused.

He's coming home, he's coming home, rejoiced Livi silently. The bust up with Rosalie has finally happened.

"Your father and I are getting divorced."

Livi felt as if a lump of cold lead had wedged between her heart and her stomach. She had yelled at her mother, cried, demanded that they think again, and throughout it all her mum had sat calmly in the armchair, explaining over and over again that it simply was not possible.

"But I *heard* Dad and Rosalie have a really bad slanging match the other day!" she persisted, in the hope that this information would change her mother's outlook. "You could still get him back, I know you could!"

Her mother smiled at her sympathetically.

"Just because people have rows, doesn't mean they're splitting up. And just because others can be civil with one another, doesn't mean they would be any good living together. I'm sorry, sweetheart, but I don't want your dad back."

"You *what?*"

Judy took a deep breath.

"I still love him, and will always wish him well and care about him but I've broken free, moved on. Things change, darling. I'm sorry."

"*You're* sorry?" Livi shouted. "How do you think I feel? I've lost my boyfriend because he turns out to be my half-brother, and now I am going to be fatherless as well!"

Judy shook her head.

"Dad will always be your dad," she said. "That's one thing that won't change. He loves you, just as I do."

"Oh yes!" Livi taunted. "Well, you've both got a very odd way of showing it! And if you're not prepared to fight for Dad, then I am!"

And she rushed out of the room, grabbed her jacket and wrenched open the front door.

"I'm going to get this whole mess sorted out once and for all!" she shouted.

hard facts

"Livi! I thought I might be seeing you. Come in."

Rosalie stepped back to let Livi through into the hall.

"Where's Dad?" snarled Livi, refusing to bestow any of the social niceties on this woman. And to think she had actually come close to liking her.

"He's gone away for a few days," said Rosalie quietly. "Coffee?"

Without waiting for an answer, she filled the kettle and put some chocolate biscuits on a plate.

"What do you mean, gone away?"

A ray of hope illuminated Livi's misery. Perhaps he'd changed his mind after all.

Rosalie poured water into two mugs and sat down opposite Livi.

"I imagine your mum has told you about their decision," she ventured. "Well . . ."

"Yes, and I suppose you think you're so

clever!" hissed Livi.

Rosalie continued as if she had not heard the interruption.

"I told Mike to go away and sort himself out," she said. "I have to be sure that it really is me that he wants—and he has to be sure, too. No woman wants to be with a guy who would rather be somewhere else."

Livi thought. Much as it pained her to admit it, there was a lot of sense in that.

"But Dad shouldn't ever have thought about being anywhere else," she protested. "And he wouldn't have done if you hadn't seduced him!"

Rosalie smiled.

"Do you know what I think has happened?" she said. "You've put your dad on a pedestal— and that's great because you love him and he's a great father and he's always been someone you've looked up to."

Livi nodded.

"However, the problem with putting someone on a pedestal is that when they fall off, it hurts them and you. Your dad is worried that you will hate him forever, and you're worried that if he is with me, he will cease to be your dad. And neither of those things are going to happen, are they?"

Livi shook her head slowly.

"Now then," said Rosalie briskly, "I'm not going to start the bit about us being bosom buddies, but I hope we can at least be civil with each other. I know right now you hate me but . . ."

Livi decided that it was time to be totally honest.

"I don't actually," she said. "I don't hate you at all."

Rosalie went pink and bit her lip.

"Are you coming to the concert?" said Livi. "It would be nice if you did."

a step forward

There couldn't be many people, thought Livi, as she stood with the others on the stage during the final curtain call of the concert, who had their mother, father, half-brother, mother's demented lodger, and father's mistress all sitting in the audience stamping and cheering. But then her gaze fell on Hayley's mum and dad and attending spouses, half and step siblings and she realised that, after all, she wasn't that different from anybody else.

The concert had been a triumph. Several of the parents were seen to dab their eyes with tissues when Hayley, as an impoverished factory girl, sang her "Please, sir, teach me to read" song and the audience had demanded an encore when Livi played a tear-jerking funereal piece as the ghost children assembled on the staircase.

After all the congratulations were over, and Mr. Golding had made a speech and thanked the parents for their ongoing support. Livi's parents and Leonora and Ryan and Rosalie stood awkwardly eyeing one another.

"Well now," said Judy, putting her arm round Livi. "Why don't I take you for a pizza?"

"How about coming with us for a Chinese?" offered her dad at precisely the same moment.

There was an awkward silence.

"I know," said Livi, hoping against hope that she was doing the right thing. "Why don't we all go for a curry?"

Judy gave a thin smile, took a deep breath and swallowed.

"That sounds like fun," interjected Livi's dad. "Let's all go together."

"I wasn't exactly sold on that idea of yours," said Judy when they got home. "But it really did help to break the ice."

"Talking of ice," said Leonora, "how about a gin?"

"You've already had three glasses of wine," admonished Livi.

"There speaks the voice of reason," sighed Leonora. "I'll go and put the kettle on."

At that moment, the phone rang.

"Who can that be, at this time of night?" said Judy.

"If you answer it, you'll find out," suggested Livi, and went into the kitchen to get a drink.

Two seconds later, there was a loud shriek.

"You don't mean it? Really? You're not pulling my leg?"

Leonora looked at Livi. "Sounds like good news."

Judy burst into the kitchen.

"I can't believe it!" she cried. "This is just amazing!"

Leonora and Livi waited expectantly.

"My gnomes," explained Judy. "The Potting Shed have sold the lot. They want more. Regularly. They want me to go to London to sign a deal. Oooh!"

And she swept Livi and then Leonora into a big hug.

"That settles it!" said Leonora.

"What?" asked Judy looking puzzled.

"We're having that gin," said Leonora.

conclusions

Miracles, Livi decided, do happen. She had spent a whole hour working out how to persuade her mother to take her along on the trip to London and in the event, her mother had simply agreed that it would be a splendid idea and why didn't they make a great occasion of it?

So they had been shopping in Harvey Nicholls, where Livi's disappointment over her inability to afford anything had evaporated in the excitement of seeing Joanna Lumley buying stockings. Then they explored the King's Road and ended up at Fables for a late lunch, which Judy couldn't eat because she was so nervous about her meeting. She had been so worried about arriving late that they got to the little shop in Beaufort Street half an hour early and had to sit on a wall out of sight until the appointed time.

"You must be Judy Joplin!" said an elegant

woman with corn-coloured hair cut into an immaculate bob and earrings the size of duck eggs.

"I am," smiled Judy. "And this is my daughter, Olivia. Livi, this is Cordelia's partner, Vanessa Cross."

They shook hands.

"Now, while we talk shop, why don't I get my daughter to take you up into the flat? I'm sure it will be more interesting than listening to us discussing discounts!" She picked up an intercom.

"Sophie! Can you come down a minute?"

The girl who appeared from the back of the shop was wearing the very pair of black lace hipsters that Livi had coveted for weeks. She also had bright purple nail polish, a figure to die for, and huge dark eyes. Livi, who had been thinking she looked moderately OK in her black A-line dress with her new tartan tights and Doc Martens actually began to feel rather drab. This girl would probably think she was a real dork.

"Hi!" said Sophie smiling broadly. "I'm the rescue service—once my mum gets into talking business, you're likely to die of galloping boredom!"

Livi laughed.

"Come on," said Sophie. "You've come at just the right time. You can help me varnish my toenails."

Livi was captivated. She had never met anyone like Sophie. She was obviously hugely rich—you only had to look at her vast bedroom with its colour TV, bedside telephone, and designer bed linen to see that. Her wardrobe rail was positively groaning under the weight of clothes and when she opened her drawer to find some nail polish, Livi saw an array of creams and potions and make-up, none of which came from Sainsbury's. Yet despite all this affluence, Sophie had no airs or graces, and was the easiest person in the world to get on with.

"You don't mind doing this, do you?" she asked, sticking a foot under Livi's nose as she painted her big toe. "Only I get them all smudged and I'm going out tonight with this divine guy, and I've got these wicked peep toe shoes, you know, all fifties—I'll show you." And she leapt up, sending the bottle of varnish flying and smudging all Livi's good work.

They looked at one another and burst out laughing. It was the sort of giggling that starts because something funny happens and continues until no one can remember what they are laughing about.

Two hours later, when Judy and Vanessa came to fetch them, they both knew they had been destined to meet.

"Mum, can Livi come and stay sometime?" pleaded Sophie. "Do you know she has never been to Planet Hollywood or South Molton Street or Covent Garden and I want to take her to Camden Market and the . . ."

Vanessa held up a hand.

"Of course she can come any time she likes," she said, as if entertaining a total stranger for the weekend was a perfectly normal occurrence. "I have a feeling that Judy is going to be visiting London quite a lot. She's heading for the big time."

* * *

"Life," said Livi as they made their way back to the Underground, "can be very odd."

Judy laughed.

"You're learning," she said. "What prompted that deep piece of philosophy?"

"Well," said Livi, "if Ryan hadn't turned out to be Dad's son, Cordelia might never have come to the house and seen your stuff, and you would never have got this contract, and I would never have met Sophie."

"True," agreed Judy. "It would be good for you to have another really close mate—help you get over Ryan."

Livi looked at her.

"I think Leonora had a point," she said.

Judy looked at her questioningly.

"Boys," said Livi. "Who needs them?"

glossary

A levels: Advanced-Level examinations, exams to receive high school diploma

Advert: advertisement

Agony Aunt/Uncle: advice columnist

Bin: garbage can

Bonnet: hood of the car

Brill: brilliant, wonderful

Chuffed: psyched, smugly pleased

Comprehensive: public school

Cred: reputation

Crisps: potato chips

Daft: stupid

Flat: apartment

GCSE's: senior exams to pass eleventh grade

Gear: clothes, belongings

Git: jerk

Gobsmacked: shocked

Go spare: freak out

Grotty: gross, dirty

Kit: gear

Loo: bathroom

Mad: crazy

Made redundant: fired, laid off
Mate: friend
Mocks: practice exams
Naff: dorky, cheesy
Poxy: disgusting
Prang: accident
Prat: fool
PSE class: Personal and Social Education class
Public school: private school
Pulling: trying to pick someone up, hitting on
Queue: line
Revision: studying for tests and exams
Riposte: reply
Row: fight
Rubbish: garbage
Ruck: scuffle, fight
Rucksack: backpack
Semi: semi-detached house
Set: class
Slagging off: criticizing
Stone: 14 lbs.
Suss: find, figure out
Uni: university
Weedy: dorky
Wet: feeble, clueless